RAID

THE RAID TEAM

Thanks to the JIT Readers

Jeff Eaton
Jeff Goode
Diane L. Smith
John Ashmore
Dave Hicks
Larry Omans

If I've missed anyone, please let me know!

Editor
The Skyhunter Editing Team

DEDICATION

To Family, Friends and
Those Who Love
to Read.
May We All Enjoy Grace
to Live the Life We Are
Called.

CHAPTER ONE

"So, do you think we're in trouble?" Jensen Pope asked the organization's council leader jokingly. Juro Sasaki's lips were pursed and showed more annoyance than amusement at the comment. Unfazed by the man's attitude, he took another look around the dark, stark room only illuminated by a few glowstrips along the ceiling. "It's odd that all the council members were called in and our leader isn't anywhere to be seen." He motioned with his head to the northern wall, where Dario leaned against it and gazed at the floor with a casual smile on his face. "But his personal assassin is."

"That's enough, Jensen." Juro hissed a sharp intake of breath. "You know we have made considerable progress toward the mission. Our leader would not need to—"

"You seem rather tense, Juro." The councilman was cut off by Xiulan Liu, the medical corporate leader, and she placed a hand on his shoulder. "Do you care to share?"

"It seems he's merely rising to Jensen's provocations again." Damyen Orlov, the Russian ark academy chancellor chuckled where he sat across the table. He sipped casually on his glass of water. "Do you lack so much stimulation, Jensen, that you must do this at every meeting?"

"It was an honest question," the man stated in his defense and looked at the other nine council members once more. "I can't be the only one thinking it, and everyone is so quiet. Even Qiana looks worried."

"Mr. Rayne isn't the kind of person to dispose of useful individuals." The entire group looked at Dario, who still stared at the ground. "Don't worry yourselves too much. Not unless you consider yourself useless. In which case, that kind of humility may spare you. Although we are supposed to be a 'secret' organization…" He looked up and tapped his chin. "How do you feel about a lobotomy instead of termination?"

Before they could retort, a holoscreen appeared in the middle of the table, and they all turned their attention to the display. Merrick looked at the group as Dario pushed himself off the wall and walked closer. "All are present, Dario?"

"Yes, indeed, *capo*." The assassin nodded and seated himself. "How have you been? We haven't talked in a couple of weeks."

"Busy, as I'm sure all of you have been," their leader stated, although his gaze had moved to look at something on his desk. "I wanted to take a moment to congratulate you all on your work thus far. We are drawing ever closer to our goal. But before we can truly begin, I need to confirm some of the particulars." His gaze darted to General Nolan Pocock, who stiffened slightly under his gaze. "General, the army—how is it coming?"

The man stood and coughed to clear his throat while he retrieved a tablet. "The droid division has been bolstered significantly and continues to grow. However, the soldier division, even with assistance from Mr. Orlov and Dario, still falls considerably short of the requisite numbers."

"Still? That's been your main priority for three years now, General," Qiana muttered. "Why not simply supplement the meat with gang members and hired mercs? I have lists of those with loose morals who would work for adequate pay."

"I've been over this with you and Ms. Liu," Nolan retorted. "We need more than merely bodies. Our targets will have no problem in dealing with mindless foot soldiers. The droids will work as a main force but for specialized matters, we need specialists."

"My robotics division has made great headway in the functionality of some of our specialist models, General," Oliver Solos offered and his gaze moved from the general to the leader. "If it comes down to it, perhaps we can use this opportunity as a proper field test."

"Field test?" Damyen mocked and shook his head. "On the day? Get your head out of your ass. You're underestimating the situation, Solos."

"Am I? Part of the human force is composed of your trainees, correct?" he asked. "Do you expect them to be prepared to fight an army of highly skilled soldiers after training for half the time or less than their adversaries?"

"Unlike that Academy, I don't coddle my students," Damyen stated and thumped the glass in his hand on the table, seemingly for emphasis. "Between my methods and the adjustments we made to our own Animus system, they will be more than formidable."

"I'm sure they will, Mr. Orlov," Nolan said, his tone placating. "But they are only a force of two hundred at the moment. That might suffice for the initial invasion, along with the number of golems we will have available, but we have to worry about the fallout and continued operations after that success. I've been able to pull some strings on my end and obtain the assistance of a private military contractor to handle the distraction objective, albeit in a way that I find somewhat tasteless."

Merrick turned to the general, intrigued. "Oh? How is that, General?"

He put the tablet down and rubbed his temples. "They want to create a smokescreen and have men go in under the guise of terrorists. The assumption is that the WC will think it is a coordinated attack by a joint operation between Black Lake and a few other groups."

"I see." The leader leaned back and closed his eyes. "We shall...consider it, for the time being. I also believe this may be contrary to what we are trying to achieve. This should be a time of unification among the human race. To use such a tactic could be—"

"Fun?" Dario interjected and earned glares from the entire table, including his boss. He held his hand up. "I suppose it would be a problem. But we have already signed up for the long haul. Even if this all goes perfectly, we won't change the hearts and minds of everyone, not until the real threat presents itself on their doorstep. I would suggest that causing a little chaos to make sure our first strike succeeds without a hitch would be a fine compromise."

"Which is why I said I would consider it," Merrick stated and returned his attention to the general. "Although, if you can think of another idea that would be suitable, Nolan, I would happily change course."

"I'll do my best, sir. As it stands, however, it may be the best option with our current forces." He sighed.

"Why not go with the lady's suggestion?" Dario asked and folded his arms. "Gang members can be quite resourceful. After all, one of our facilities was destroyed by a former gang member."

Damyen turned to Dario and sneered. "You say that so casually for the idiot who lost it in the first place."

"Too true," he conceded. "But it did open my eyes to the possibilities. It wasn't a huge loss for us at this point. But for such a small team to succeed, maybe there are others like him we could have at our disposal?"

"You're letting your bloodlust show, Dario." Xiulan huffed. "And making connections where there aren't any. Whatever his past may be, that was a team of trained Nexus students."

"Half-trained," Oliver countered. "They were third years."

"And the one who destroyed your droid in that junk town last year was a second year," Jensen added and kicked his feet onto the table. "Damn shame about that. I had to put a fair amount of work in myself to try to smokescreen it all."

"Which is why you should have used your own men to make the robbery instead of relying on that Halo gang,"

Oliver snapped and he frowned at the normally calm man's sudden rage. "I believe that shows the kind of competence we can expect should we hire those kinds of ruffians."

"So, we're going with no, then?" Dario asked and twiddled his thumbs. "It's a shame, really. There'll be so much unused stock without hands to hold those weapons."

"We'll send those to my contact before the time comes if I cannot amass a larger army," Nolan stated and stared at Dario before he turned to the leader. "And I promise you, sir, nothing like that incident will ever happen again. I have made sure that all our remaining facilities are well guarded. They won't have a prayer of getting in."

"We're in," Kaiden stated triumphantly and kicked a dented droid head down the hall as he made his way into the base. His armor was mostly shattered and his shields depleted. He held Sire in one hand and a stolen machine gun in the other. His visor was cracked, as well, and he contemplated simply peeling it out before he proceeded.

"It took you longer to get in here than it takes you to complete some missions," Chief noted. *"And I'm picking up a hell-ton of signals. I think—"*

Three mechanicals fell from above and unfolded to reveal themselves as Havoc droids with cannons on each arm. The ace readied to fight and aimed both weapons at the bots before a thud behind him drew his attention. He glanced over his shoulder as the heavy doors of the entrance closed behind him. "I thought you said you had access to their systems?"

"*I do— did! I didn't even realize I was overwritten,*" the EI stated. More droids—four, seven, then fifteen—landed in front of them. He held Sire's trigger down as they began to approach. "*To finish my thought, I was going to say I think you might have overdone it.*"

CHAPTER TWO

Explosions erupted in the hall. Kaiden powered his way through a door farther in, the droids in hot pursuit while turrets activated as he continued to race deeper into the facility. His left arm had given out and his legs were hardly sturdy anymore. *Keep going. Keep fighting.* He maintained the inner chant and simply didn't have the time to think of much else at this point. Sire responded to the slight adjustment in his aim and destroyed two turrets as he made his way into a hangar.

The ace looked around for another door or elevator he could use, but all he saw was a ladder that led to the catwalk above. He turned and shot the terminal at the entrance door, which immediately began to close as the Havoc and Soldier droids behind him began to fire. They blew the doors open before they even had a chance to close fully. Kaiden swore quietly as he holstered Sire, hauled himself up the ladder, and dropped his last thermals behind him as he scrambled higher. A searing pain stabbed in his back a second before he reached the top. With a grimace, he crawled onto the platform as the explosives detonated. Droids didn't seem to have much self-preservation instinct, but with how many there were, that seemed moot at this point.

He fumbled behind him and his fingers touched singed flesh. Even though the underlay had dispersed the majority of the shots, the blasts had burnt deeply into him. He had almost forgotten what it was like to feel a direct strike like that. It was sobering, but he would worry about it later. He pushed himself up and raced across the catwalk while he drew Sire to fire at the droids below that continued to file in.

A door at the end of the platform probably led into the next hangar. One of them would have a route somewhere else eventually. He prepared to fire at the panel to force the door but it opened on its own—not for him but for the Assault droids behind it. Kaiden skidded to a halt and instinctively raised his rifle to fire before it was shot out of his hand by a Soldier droid below. He grimaced as he reached for Debonair, but the Assault droids' guns had already primed and a hail of laser fire rocketed toward him.

The sensation of taking multiple strikes wouldn't be easily forgotten. His body was torn apart when white-hot projections of energy seared into his shoulder, torso, legs, and stomach. He collapsed and blood pooled and dripped from the walkway. How was he still conscious? Perhaps the better question was how he could be alive at all. He didn't have to worry about that for long, however. Metallic clanks approached along the walkway and a white light began to appear in his peripheral vision. He clenched his teeth as the Assault droid ahead of him raised a leg and brought it down as the light consumed his vision.

Kaiden gasped as his pod opened and he fell out to land awkwardly with a loud thud. He coughed for a moment before he crumpled into himself as the pain from the Animus wracked his body. This had turned out to be a bad start to the day.

"Damn, you were fucked up in there, partner," Chief commented.

"I noticed." He groaned and winced as he rolled onto his back. Something poked painfully into his ribs—not one of the many needles that seemed to stab relentlessly into his body but more of a dull impact like someone was kicking him.

"Are you all right?" a soft voice asked. He blinked a few times before his vision cleared enough to see Chiyo kneeling beside him. She probed his cheek gently. "I had assumed that at this point, you might be accustomed to pain."

"I am, but it's still not a friend," the ace muttered and slapped her hand away. "Quit it! You're literally kicking me while I'm down right now."

"Because I'm sure that's much worse than becoming a trypophobic's nightmare due to a multitude of lasers." She sighed, stood, and offered a hand. He stretched automatically to take it before a new wave of pain made him stiffen and he closed his hand and held a finger up.

"I'm gonna lay here for a while. Is that all right?" he asked and huddled into himself again as she sighed and sat.

"I guess there's not much of a choice for now," she muttered and studied him for a moment. "You know, I watched on the console and I looked up the specs you chose. We were supposed to do that mission together and even with the two of us, that would have been way too much."

"Have some faith, Chi." He grimaced and began to rub his chest when he coughed a couple of times.

"If this is how you see faith, you must be the equivalent of one of the self-flagellating monks." She sighed. "Kaiden, you know the map Laurie designed for us is only based on our best guess of what their facility could be like. Even if there are only half of the forces we think there are, we could bring all our friends and still not have a chance to do any real damage."

Kaiden dragged in a deep breath, rolled onto his back again, and stretched, taking slow, measured breaths as he inclined his head to look at her. "Sasha and Laurie won't let us, remember? They say we can't offer it to contracted students."

"I'm simply giving an example," she stated. "What was your plan, exactly? Simply to see how long you could survive on a suicide run?"

"Well, like you said, we were supposed to do it together, but you took so long that I decided to go solo to get an understanding of the floor plan and all that. I wanted to see if I could make enough time for you to work your hacking magic, shut them down, or gain control or something like that."

She rolled her eyes. "Kaiden, first off, the design isn't one-to-one. It's based on what we know so far. Much of the information still needs to be decrypted, and there's no real map of the location. I wouldn't know where to go without scouting first. Even if I did, it took you thirty minutes to even step foot in there—and only ten to die. That's not anywhere near enough time for me."

He winced as he shrugged. "I'll make sure to die slower."

"And I was running late because I did some investigating this morning—the kind you asked me to do," she reminded him.

His eyes widened. "Oh, right, damn. Uh...sorry. Did you manage to find any of them?"

Chiyo shook her head. "All the people you asked me to look into came up with nothing other than some generic info for civilians who shared names. I assume they went off the grid or joined merc companies and moved on."

The ace frowned and focused his gaze on the ceiling. "I guess the Dead-Eyes are living up to the first part of the name, but there was only a couple of dozen left anyway. I guess I shouldn't give them a hard time for wanting to move on."

She looked away. While he didn't show it now, he had seemed a little emotional when he asked her to find members of his old gang. It must have weighed heavily on him that he never decided to look into them himself and that such a big part of his life was gone.

"*Madame, you have a message from the professor,*" Kaitō stated from her EI pad.

Chief appeared above Kaiden and stared at him. "*Partner, Laurie's looking for you.*"

He closed his eyes at the sudden bright light. "I need to get you one of those pads and keep you tucked away at times like these."

The EI's eye furrowed angrily. *"I don't want one of those glorified fishbowls."*

"I find it quite a suitable abode, myself," Kaitō interjected.

Chief turned an ashen grey and shook for a moment before he refocused. *"Get moving. It looks important,"* he stated before he disappeared.

Kaiden sat and rolled his shoulders. "He's called us both in, so I guess this must be about the AO."

"We won't know until we see him," Chiyo pointed out and looked at the message on her pad. "But it seems to be with how cryptic he's being. Let's go."

She helped him up and he cursed quietly until he was on his feet and took a moment to stretch. "Do you mind if I stop at Dr. Soni's before we go? I need a dose of K-brew to make the day chipper."

"The fact that it's named after you means you use it too much," she chided and dragged him along. "Walk it off. We have a meeting at the auditorium later, remember?"

"Can't we skip it? We already know about the final," he pleaded and walked almost as robotically as the droids he had recently battled.

"Consider this part of your lesson," she stated and continued down the hall.

"What lesson?" he asked.

Chiyo stopped at the top of the stairs and fixed him with a firm look. "Never do something foolish without me there to help you." Without waiting for his response, she spun and resumed her determined stride.

He chuckled. "She could have worded that better."

"At least I don't have to shoulder it myself anymore," Chief added.

"Yeah, yeah." He looked at the steps and his legs flared with pain simply at the sight. "Fuck that. Which way to the elevators?"

CHAPTER THREE

The two friends entered Laurie's office. Kaiden still tried to stretch his strained appendages and eased his neck for the umpteenth time as he called to the professor.

"We're here, Laurie. You know, you can simply ping us instead of—" He stopped when his gaze settled on a rather large figure seated in his usual chair. "Wolfson?"

"Hey, boyo." The head officer grunted and looked lazily at him but frowned when he noted his odd posture. "What's wrong with you?"

"Failed Animus mission," Chiyo answered calmly and took the chair opposite the giant.

Wolfson smirked, shook his head, and kicked his feet onto Laurie's table. "Failing missions in your third year? Come on now, Kaiden. That's not a good precedent to set now that you're only a few months away from being a Victor."

The ace wobbled over to one of the couches in the

lounge and sat gingerly. "I was running through a simulation that Laurie made about the AO facility."

"A very early simulation that is not even close to complete that you pushed for, I should remind you." The professor huffed and strained to push his colleague's large boots off the table. "And I would thank you to not scuff my table."

"I can be delicate when the situation calls for it. I'm not saying it does now, but the hope is there." Wolfson chuckled and returned his attention to the ace. "So, you wanted to have a look at the facility. What did you find?"

"A crap-load of droids," he muttered and laid down. "It was as if I was being hunted by every droid in the Death Match simultaneously. I ended up gunned down by a team of Assaults."

"What was the point, then?" Wolfson asked. "To see if you could wreck an entire production facility on your own?"

"I was testing something," he explained and looked at Chiyo, who was asking if she could have tea while Laurie continued to stare daggers at the giant. "According to some, I would have been more help simply streaking through as quickly as possible."

"I made no such insinuation," his friend retorted quietly as she went over to a tea heater near Laurie's desk.

"Either way, it was foolish to attempt it on your own, Kaiden," the professor reprimanded him. "I made the map empty on purpose. It was only for reconnaissance. To have changed the settings and turned it into a death trap like that, your instincts should be far sharper than they are."

"So, you were watching then?" he asked.

"We certainly were." Wolfson chuckled. "I was surprised to see any parts of you left by the end."

"You too? Then why did you ask what was wrong with me?" he asked and raised his head to stare at his instructor.

"I wanted to hear you admit it." He laughed. "Humility is healthy every once and a while."

"I wish you would demonstrate 'every once and a while,'" he muttered and turned his attention to Laurie. "Did you call us here for a reason, or is this simply a lecture?"

"If that was the case, I wouldn't have asked Chiyo to join us," the man retorted and turned his monitor. "I wish you had more patience. If you had, you wouldn't have bothered to use the current map because Aurora and I have found a new one."

"Their HQ?" Kaiden asked and bolted upright in excitement despite his stiffness. "Where is it?"

"I don't think it's their main base," the professor clarified as he opened the file and displayed the blueprints for a large facility. "Despite that, it's built like a stronghold. It's definitely of some importance to them. My guess is that it's some kind of off-site storage facility or barracks, maybe even a lab."

"Perhaps a little of all of them," Chiyo suggested as she studied the diagram. "The assassin didn't label them, but a few of the rooms are circled with symbols in each. I assume they are a personal code."

"I agree, but that brings me to my next point—or question, rather." Laurie looked at Kaiden. "When we agreed on this venture, you said you had an idea where you could get additional forces. How is that coming along, dear Kaiden?"

The ace glanced quickly at Chiyo and assumed a solemn expression. "Let's go with slowly." He sighed and leaned back. "But I guess, looking at it now, even if my idea had worked out, we still wouldn't have had nearly enough men to raid something that big."

"From the looks of it, the number of hostiles you faced in the Animus is actually a safer estimate than I thought," the infiltrator admitted and grimaced while she flipped through the various blueprints and a few hazy pictures. "I'm not sure if there's a production component to this building or not, but there are a considerable number of droids and even some of those golems."

Kaiden closed his eyes to think without distraction. He needed more men if he wanted to actually accomplish this, but he consistently drew a blank. Aside from anything else, he certainly didn't have the credits to hire a merc force—not that he wanted to, even if he had the means to hire one of the right caliber.

"Hey, Wolfson," he called. "Do you know anyone who would like to eliminate a shadowy doomsday group?"

"Not offhand. Most of my buddies are retired or... Well, they can't join for obvious reasons." He shrugged and it was clear he wouldn't expand any further.

"Not even Raza?"

"He's back on his homeworld, dealing with some kind of ritual event. He couldn't come even if he wanted to, and despite the warp gate, it would take him a few days. From the sounds of it, though, you don't even have a plan."

"What about you?" he suggested. "You have some skin in this, don't you?"

"I certainly do." He nodded and craned his neck over

the back of his chair to look at Kaiden, who had moved closer to the blueprints. "I intended to go with you, whether you suggested it or not, but from the sounds of it, you are simply going on a suicide mission that will accomplish nothing. So, for now, my job is to make sure you keep your happy ass here until you do make a slightly reasonable suggestion."

"So that's why you're here—to metaphorically sit on me," Kaiden complained.

Wolfson scoffed, removed his feet from the table, and stood. "Try something foolish and it will be literal."

"He already has, technically," Chiyo interjected.

"You've both made your point." The ace huffed and ran a hand through his hair. "I'll think of something. I won't let this opportunity pass me by."

"You're not in this alone, Kaiden," Laurie reminded him. "We all want to succeed and expose the organization and its activities. But as it stands, our hands are tied and we don't want to lose one of our best students when it's actually in our hands now."

"I know. That's why you offered to make something up for our final," he responded and closed his eyes wearily.

Ringing sounded in his head and from Chiyo's pad. He opened his eyes to read a message.

All Masters, please report to the auditorium for your finals seminar.

"Well, speaking of which…" Chiyo smirked, put the pad away, and finished her tea.

"Do we have to go?" Kaiden sighed and sank into a nearby chair. "We already know the gist of it, and we have our target squared away."

"It's mandatory, Kaiden," she reminded him, walked over, and extended a hand to help him up.

"You're contract-free like me so don't have to be a teacher's pet anymore," he grumbled but took her hand and allowed her to haul him to his feet.

"That's a good point," she stated and released him without warning. He lost his balance and toppled into an untidy heap and she grinned.

"Son of a… Daughter of a… Dammit!" he stammered as he forced himself up and glared at her with a mixture of pain and annoyance. "Funny, Chi."

"I agree," she said with a small smile. "We're going so the others don't worry, and there's something Genos wanted to ask as well."

"Genos? What does he want?"

"You'll learn at the auditorium." She made no effort to elaborate and shooed him toward the door where she paused and turned to address Laurie with a bow. "Thank you for notifying us, Professor."

The ace gave a lazy wave. "Yeah, appreciate ya. I'll think of something and be back soon," he promised as they stepped out of the office.

Professor Laurie sighed and turned his monitor to study his findings. "I certainly hope so, my boy."

CHAPTER FOUR

The auditorium was abuzz with the third years chatting amongst themselves. Kaiden had to admit he wasn't as swept up in it as he had been in previous years. For one thing, he knew what lay ahead—to the letter, in fact, as Laurie had explained it all. What he was more interested in was what Genos had to say. Chiyo had made it sound rather cryptic. Had his Tsuna friend done something wrong? Did he need help? He would certainly lend a hand with whatever his friend needed, but Genos knew he wasn't exactly the one to call for delicate matters.

As the duo entered the side door that led into the balcony, he looked over the railing to the Tsunas' section. At this point, it was only partially filled with more coming in, but the integration had been more and more successful, so most actually filed into the room amongst the general populace. He didn't see Genos or Jaxon. They must already be with the group.

"It's good to see you, Kaiden." A firm hand slapped his shoulder and he turned to see Flynn's wide smile. "You too,

Chi. Did you just get here? Come on. Everyone is waiting for us."

The three of them continued to the balcony. Marlo and Mack greeted one another with a firm handshake that seemed to evolve—devolve?—into an arm-wrestling match. Luke, his grin wide, jogged over to referee. Izzy waved at Chiyo while Silas and Otto greeted the trio as they entered. The entire group was together except for their Tsuna buddies. The ace frowned and wondered if they'd chosen not to join them.

"Greetings, friends!" Kaiden whipped around at the familiar voice and smiled when Genos and Jaxon appeared from the opposite stairwell. The group greeted the two while he made his way over to them.

"How ya doing, Genos?" he asked, grasped his hand, and all but dragged him over to Chiyo.

"Hello, friend Kaiden. You seem rather eager. Also, your movements seem a little stiff," the mechanist noted.

"I was blasted this morning but I'm getting better," he responded and ignored a twinge of pain in his shoulder. He was improving slowly but surely. "I wanted to speak to you —or, rather, I heard you wanted to speak to me."

"Ah, yes, that. Certainly. We should have some time before the speech begins." Genos nodded and sat beside Chiyo while Kaiden settled next to him. "I suppose I should begin right away. I have heard of your plans from friend Chiyo." He nodded to the infiltrator.

Chiyo? It wasn't like her to spill secrets and he thought they were supposed to keep this quiet. He looked at her, puzzled.

"He had already decided something was off," she

explained. "We never said anything about the drive after we gave it to the Academy. His team was the one who recovered it."

"I didn't want to pry. But after she told me what you were planning…well, I want you to know first that I haven't told the others. Friend Chiyo did tell me it was a sensitive matter. However, I want to tell you that I wish to help."

Kaiden frowned. It was a kind offer, but if Chiyo had filled him in, he should know all that it would entail. "I know you have been given orders to not involve us," the Tsuna stated and gestured to the group behind him. "But I am offering on my own behalf with no coercion or even an invitation from either of you. That should be a…loophole in your contract correct?"

He regarded his friend with new respect. Genos displayed a rather wily side, which was a little out of character for him, but he could see the determination in his eyes. This wasn't him trying to be cheeky but wanting to help and coming up with a way to circumvent the contract was merely a part of it. The ace nodded, but before he could reply, the lights dimmed and the stage illuminated. Holoscreens appeared on the front of the balcony with Chancellor Durand's face and smile filling the display. A look through the translucent screens confirmed that the chancellor now stepped to the podium on the stage.

"Good morning, students." He greeted them cheerfully. "You know the date and that the end of your master year is coming up, which means this meeting is for one thing and one thing only. Discussion of your upcoming finals."

Well, that and the message they received before the conference, although that had only been he and Chiyo.

"This is the big one. I would argue that this is the test of greatest importance—even more so then next year's," Durand continued. "That may sound odd, but I'm sure you all know that next year's rank is dubbed 'Victor,' a signifier of your goal. To be victorious and strive for success. When you graduate, it will have true meaning. As such, this year's final is proof that you are prepared to take on the tasks that await you once you graduate."

The chancellor looked around the room. Despite his earlier smile, he seemed much more stern than normal. Still, there was a trust in his gaze that Kaiden recognized and he was sure others could see it as well. "We know that after last year's incident, some are concerned that there may be other 'complications.' I give you my word now, exactly as I did at the beginning of the year, that nothing will befall you." His face turned solemn for a moment before it relaxed again as quickly. "At least, I can promise that as long as you stay here. But to show that you are prepared for the dangers that await you outside of this island, you must face reality—a rather loaded word in this case."

He looked off-stage and nodded at someone in the wings. "This year, your finals will not take place in the Animus but in the world itself."

His face faded from the holoscreens, which now displayed the profiles of the various students, teachers, and faculty members as they appeared and disappeared in rapid succession.

"All of you will take part in a mission in teams of two to four," he announced

"Oh, we have this made." Flynn chuckled and glanced at Kaiden, who merely shrugged. The marksman was certainly right for himself and the others. He, however, was less sure about his chances for obvious reasons.

"You will go out and find a mission for yourself and your team to complete. You may either locate them yourself—something I'm sure a few of you are accustomed to." He could swear the chancellor glanced his way. While he had never really interacted with the man, did he know about his off-island work? He was probably only being paranoid.

The crowd began to chatter in surprise. "You can also receive missions from many of the teachers and faculty here. But don't think it will be a cake-walk. Each faculty member has had to pre-screen their mission to make sure it is worthy for future victors to undertake. For that matter, don't think you can simply go out and complete some easy retrieval mission or D-rank merc gig and have that count. You have trained to be the best. Strive to find a mission that will prove it."

Durand took a deep breath as the lights of the theater dimmed further. "This is a gauge of the application of your talents, a way to get the most out of your abilities, to learn and implement teamwork, and to see how you fare against unique and often dangerous adversaries or situations. The kind many of you will face in the years to come once you have graduated."

"He's really hammering that home, isn't he?" Cameron muttered.

"Things have been getting way more real for all of us recently," Silas agreed and his gaze drifted over the students below them. "I'm not exactly a people person, but even if the rest of the school hasn't gone through what we have, they've had to deal with their own issues, I'm sure."

"Kid gloves are off now," Mack added.

Izzy shook her head. "I don't think they've ever been on. Now, it's brass knuckles."

Dozens of holograms filled the area above them and battled each other or aided one another, while ships evaded and others were battered by storms and explosions. "Even for those of you who aren't here for the soldier course, you are Nexus students and I'm sure you've grown to understand the dangers in the world—and even the ones off it," Durand continued. "The Animus has prepared you for that and your teachers have prepared you for that. But you and your teammates must now face it. For there to be a goal, you must know what you are fighting against. You must now use all your personal skills and connections to make it through."

Personal connections… Something clicked inside Kaiden's mind. The chancellor continued to speak but it had basically become white noise to him. He was lost in thought now that the word "connections" had jolted his awareness and he realized that he'd been too close to the situation for it to really sink in before. His old gang and his friends were all important and helpful, but he needed an army—tough fighters with grit and who were willing to play dirty. He began to smile. The more he thought about it, the more sense it made and the wider his smile became. So much so, that Chiyo and Genos noticed.

"Kaiden, are you all right?" she asked.

"I'm dandy," he replied and looked at her with his wide, almost devilish smile. "But I thought of some connections I need to contact."

"Your smile is something of a concern, friend Kaiden," the Tsuna remarked and leaned back in his chair.

"Do you know what a 'eureka moment' is, Genos?" the ace asked.

Genos turned to Chiyo, who simply shrugged. "It is another term for 'epiphany,' correct?"

"Correct." He nodded. "One I get to rub in Wolfson's face once this is over."

"Um, maybe you should go see Dr. Soni once this is done," Chiyo suggested. "I think you rattled your brain along with everything else."

"*Unfortunately, no, everything is working normally up here,*" Chief confirmed, although mostly to himself as Kaiden certainly wasn't listening. "*Which is even more troubling.*"

CHAPTER FIVE

"You plan to knock on the doors of other gangs to help you?" Wolfson asked incredulously and took another swing at Kaiden, who dodged to the side. "Let me hit you and see if you're still thinking straight after that."

"Yeah, because that would make it better," he retorted and swept a leg out quickly. He caught Wolfson on the ankle but he still didn't have the strength to topple the giant. When his attempt failed, he pushed away and retreated a few steps before his leg was all but crushed by Wolfson's foot. "I have connections now. I admit there's no guarantee that all of them will say yes, but I'm sure the Fire Riders would be interested, at least."

"And how will you contact them?" his instructor asked before he barreled down on the ace, who vaulted over him and kicked off his back. The man stumbled with a grunt.

"I already contacted my gig dealer. He knows one of the Fire Rider's...dispatchers, I guess? Either way, I'll have him set us up. If I'm right, I may be able to get in touch with the Skyway Kings as well."

"You've made many assumptions, boyo." Wolfson swung an arm but Kaiden ducked beneath it before he caught his adversary in the ribcage, spun, and pounded a fist into the officer's gut. Pain surged through his hand and he stepped back and shook it, then wiggled his fingers to make sure he hadn't broken anything.

"You simply don't want to admit it's a decent plan," he accused.

The head officer stood and rubbed his side. "I'll admit, it's good, but it all comes down to whether you can make it happen. You'll certainly get your manpower if it works out, but you'll need more than muscle and guns to have a chance that this will be a success."

"I have something lined up for support, but I'm a little unsure how that one will pan out because it requires finesse."

"You are good at bullshitting," Chief interjected, although Kaiden was unsure if it was supposed to be sarcastic or oddly encouraging.

"Well, you have my blessing if that's what you're looking for." Wolfson rubbed his shoulder and raised his fists in a boxing stance. "I guess we can't be too choosy right now. I want to know what those bastards are up to."

"So you're as worried as I am that this chance may slip away?" he asked and prepared to engage once more.

"I doubt a fortress like that will suddenly up and disappear," the man responded and took small steps to the side as the two began to circle one another. "But if they've targeted us these last couple of years, that's sufficient time to make plans and preparations. I'm worried about what comes next."

As Kaiden sidestepped around the arena and moved closer to one of the tables, he sneaked his hand out and snatched two items he'd seen before the bout started. He flipped the gun in his hand while he pocketed the other, then aimed the weapon at Wolfson. "You probably should be."

He fired and his instructor charged through the force shots and hauled his arm back to deliver a punishing blow. The ace sprinted to the side and continued to fire while the giant pursued him. A well-placed shot on the edge of another table flipped it and slid the other guns out of his opponent's reach. He looked at the weapon and activated a switch that allowed for charged shots but knew it would take time to power up.

The ace held the trigger down while he slid his other hand into his pocket. When his adversary leapt forward, he pushed off the floor to slide under him as he grasped the grenade in his pocket and lobbed it back. It burst open, ensnared the goliath of a man in a net, and constricted around him as he lost his balance. Despite the restraints, the officer was able to flip himself in the air to land on his feet before the mesh began to dig into his arms and chest.

Kaiden had no desire to waste the opportunity. He twisted and fired the charged shot. A blast of pressurized air drove into Wolfson's chest to break the skin but, more importantly, knock him down. He tried to flip up again, but the younger man lunged and hammered furiously with everything he had—both the butt of his pistol and his free hand, ignoring the pain.

His instructor's face was bloody and bruised and his eyes were closed. Kaiden couldn't even tell if he was conscious or not, but it would be stupid to assume anything considering it was Wolfson. He held the trigger down once again and aimed it at his face.

"So, can I get a little humility now?" he asked and tapped the older man's face with the barrel of the gun. "I need you to be as ready as can be, and a concussion wouldn't be—"

"We've done this for over fifty matches now. Do you really think I'll give in?" Wolfson asked and spat blood onto Kaiden's face.

"I still got this," the ace stated and brandished the pistol as he wiped his face. "At this range, you won't die but it'll hurt like hell, even for you."

"Only if you hit me with it." The man huffed and glared at his trainee. "Which you should have done by now instead of gloating." In one swift motion, he headbutted his opponent and dislodged him easily. He snuck a blade from under his bracer and used it to sever the net so he could stand, rolled his shoulders, and hawked another small glob of blood,

Kaiden backed away as the giant stepped forward, taking deep breaths as he balled his fists. "Although I suppose I should say congratulations. You managed some good hits."

"And you've yet to get one solid hit in," the ace jeered with a smirk. He aimed the pistol and released the trigger. The shot caught him squarely in the left shoulder and the skin popped off with a small burst of blood. Wolfson merely looked at the wound with disinterest and grinned.

"How long do you think it will take you to get all this together?" he asked and folded his arms.

The younger man looked at him and then at the gun, shrugged, and tossed the weapon aside. "The finals start in a week. So, a week. I need to talk it over with my team first. I'll probably need Genos' help as a pilot."

"Genos? He's one of the Tsuna you hang out with, right?" Wolfson asked and wiped his lips with the back of his arm. "Didn't Sasha and Laurie say to not involve anyone else?"

"He offered. I didn't involve anyone." He looked away for a moment. "Although I'm heading over to Sasha's after this. I'll see what he has to say."

"That's probably one of your wiser moves." The officer chuckled. "If there is one thing Sasha hates it's those who openly balk his orders. He can be rather frightening when enraged."

"I don't think I've ever seen him anything other than stern, really," Kaiden commented.

"He doesn't get all shouty like most others do. In fact, it's an eerie calm. There's nothing more frightening than someone who's angry with you but has their presence of mind intact," Wolfson stated. He stroked his beard in thought and glanced around the room. "I mentioned that I don't have any reinforcements to offer other than myself. Obviously, I can't exactly order the other security officers to help. This is above their paygrade." His gaze settled on the weapons strewn about the floor. "But we'll need weapons and armor to outfit those men you hope to recruit. Something better than whatever second-hand guns and black-market tech they have. I'll see what I can whip up."

"That sounds good, thanks." He walked over to his

jacket, which hung over a chair across the room. "Hey, Wolfson…"

"Yeah, boyo?"

Kaiden pulled his jacket on and turned back. "I have to say I'm excited to work with you in the field. I only got to see you work for a short time before we were separated in that cave."

"Hunting the Lycan, I remember," the man recalled.

"Try to not fall into any pits when we head off, all right?" he joked and turned toward the door. "I'll contact you later."

Wolfson watched him go and grinned when he recalled that little side mission. Kaiden, shaken up by his near-death experience with Gin, had to get his fire going again. He thought about how his charge had changed since then and he smiled. Nothing would put that flame out again.

CHAPTER SIX

"Can I help you?" a man in the Nexus offices lobby asked but didn't sound particularly enthusiastic.

"I'm Master Kaiden Jericho," Kaiden announced. "I'm here to visit Commander Chevalier. I sent a message ahead."

The man looked at his tablet and scanned through it for a moment before he returned his attention to the ace. "I don't see your name here. You'll need to—"

The monitor on the guard's screen began to glow blue and both startled when a wire-frame owl appeared. "*Good day to the both of you,*" it said calmly.

"Hey, Isaac." Kaiden greeted in return and smiled at the guard, who merely shrugged.

"Does the commander know he's coming?" the guard asked the EI.

"*Indeed. He apologizes for not sending the clearance down. He was busy for the last half hour and just saw the message. Please allow Master Jericho to proceed to his office.*"

"Tell the commander he's on his way." The guard nodded and waved him along,

"Much appreciated, Matthew," Isaac replied before he vanished again.

"Take the elevator to the sixth floor. Your EI can guide you to his office. Head directly there and only there."

"Right." He walked briskly past the man to the elevators, called one down and entered, then pressed the key for the sixth floor. He tapped his foot while he waited for the ascent.

"So, what do you think you'll get out of him?" Chief asked.

"You make it sound like I'm shaking him down," he protested. "Like Wolfson said in Laurie's office, all three of them have a reason to want to eliminate the AO. I'm only here to tell him my plan and see what he has to say."

"And you think he'll be okay with it?" The EI sounded skeptical.

"We don't have many other options. Whichever way you look at it, we can't really go in with a small team if we want to live to talk about it." He stepped out when the elevator reached the sixth floor.

"And what about the whole Genos situation?" Chief asked.

"That might be more complicated," he admitted. "I think he should be all right with it, though. If nothing else, we can have Genos help during the recruitment process if Sasha puts his foot down. That way, he can still help but won't be involved in the main fight."

"Do you really think Genos would be happy with that?"

"Probably not, but I'd rather deal with an angry Genos than an angry commander. Especially after what Wolfson said. Someone who can spook him is not someone I want to fuck with." Kaiden rounded the corner and strode the last few steps to the commander's office. He knocked on the door and waited for a response. In a moment, a blue, glowing owl appeared above him.

"Hello again, Isaac." The EI's eyes circled in its head

"Hello again to you, Kaiden. The commander is almost finished. Please come in and make yourself at home."

"Unfortunately, I can't get drunk quite yet but I'll do my best," he joked

"Very good. Allow me to get the door." Isaac disappeared and the door opened. The room was surprisingly dark despite it being only the afternoon. A couple of lamps were on and the windows were covered.

Kaiden walked in and the door closed behind him. "Sasha, are you here?"

"Over here, Kaiden." He followed the commander's voice to a small, round table in the corner. Sasha sat in a chair with his back to him and studied something on a holoscreen. "I'm sorry I didn't see your message sooner."

"It's all right. I only wanted to touch base." He took the chair opposite, hooked an arm over the back, and inclined his head. "I've come up with a plan for the…uh, situation."

The commander raised an eyebrow. "Really, now? Do tell, and please feel free to speak your mind. No one is listening but me, I can assure you."

The ace nodded and leaned in. "I intend to rally the troops, as it were, and recruit them from some of my previous temporary alliances."

"Temporary alliances?"

"Other gangs. The Fire Riders and Skyway Kings, for example," he explained.

"I see." Sasha nodded, leaned back in his chair, and crossed one leg over the other. "Do you believe they will be receptive to this?"

"I'll have to give them some facts, obviously. Not too many, I promise, but the Fire Riders would definitely be interested. After all, Gin was hired by the AO, technically. He was a little vague about it, according to Wolfson. But both of them were at Ramses and that assassin worked for them. That should garner some interest in retaliation."

The other man nodded thoughtfully, picked up a glass of water, and sipped slowly. "What will you do if they ask for payment?"

Kaiden leaned back and scratched his head. "I thought I could tell them to strip the place when we're done and let them have anything they can carry to sell."

"That's a rather risky move. If there are high-grade weapons or tech there, you'll put it in the hands of gang members."

"The Fire Riders and Kings are basically merc groups. I won't try to get someone like the Vice Ghouls on board," he clarified. "Although, if they sell them, that could lead to some problems. And with the Halos involved—"

"Halos?" Sasha questioned. "As in the Azure Halos? When did you meet them?"

"Middle of last year, although 'met' may not exactly be the correct term," he admitted. "I'm not sure how it will go with them. There is a connection between them and AO."

"How so?"

"I infiltrated their junk town to track a droid they stole.

According to the files on that drive, it was developed by a company that has connections to the AO, potentially setting them up," he revealed. "All gangs have different rules and honor systems and all that but no one likes to be set up."

"I see. It's another risk but having a group of hackers to assist would be useful." Sasha sighed as he took another sip. "Most of my instincts tell me this is too much of a gamble—"

"But we don't have a lot of options," Kaiden interrupted and finished for him. "Most of us seem to agree on that. But until we actually have solid evidence that we can show to the world, we'll have to fight a shadowy group with shady people."

Sasha chuckled. "An apt description. I suppose." He rubbed his chin thoughtfully. "I understand your plan. Do you have anything else to add?"

Kaiden nodded and took a deep breath. "There was one new development a couple of hours ago. You see, one of my friends worked out what's going on. I'm sure a couple of others have their suspicions but this one was surprisingly pushy. His name is Genos."

"The Tsuna engineer. I know him." Sasha set his glass down. "I assume he wants to join you?"

"That's right. You see, I thought since technically, I wasn't the one who asked—"

"He can come," the commander stated flatly.

"Just like that?" He blinked in surprise. "Well, this was an easier conversation than I expected."

"Perhaps, but that's because of the situation," the other man explained and leaned closer. "I'll leave it to your discretion. You know his capabilities better than I do. At the same time, I know what tends to happen when you turn someone away who is dead set on helping others. They find a way and it can end poorly for them, unfortunately. If anything happens to him, it will be on you as not only his friend but as an ace."

He nodded and thought it over. Genos had more than proven himself as a fighter, so he would be all right. There were hard times, but he always pulled through. If he wanted to help, he couldn't turn him away simply because he feared for his safety, and the same with Chiyo. It seemed something of a dick move to ask a group of strangers to risk their lives and not trained soldiers. Being a leader was stressful.

"You know, there is one contact you haven't considered, Kaiden," Sasha noted.

The ace looked sharply at him. "Really? Who's that?"

His companion looked thoughtfully at his monitor. "Well, he's the reason you have the freedom you do now, and he also has his own score to settle with the organization. He made a promise to help if you ever needed it as well," he hinted, and Kaiden's eyes widened when a face came to mind. Before he could say the name, Sasha continued. "I'll look into it and get back to you. And I should let you know that if all goes well, I'll be at your side when you storm the castle."

Instinctively, his gaze drifted to the wall where the commander's rifle hung in a frame near a bookcase. The man knew how to shoot. He'd seen that in the Animus. It had probably been a while since he took it out of that case in the real world, though. "Thanks, Commander."

"You're not alone in this. Remember that, Jericho. And don't forget what you are, either."

"I won't," he promised and focused on a certificate on the desk—the man's graduation certificate from Nexus bearing their shared class. "I'm an ace and I'll hold myself to that."

CHAPTER SEVEN

"You think the weather will be this nice when we actually attack?" Chiyo asked, her gaze on the twilight skies above.

"To be honest, I wonder if the enemy forces will be this neglectful," Kaiden admitted. He perched near the edge of the hillside and peered at the tall fortress below. "I've simply stared at them quite openly for nearly ten minutes now and not really tried to be incognito at all. You'd think someone would have noticed us by now."

"They haven't because I changed the map rules to only be in spectator mode," Cyra, Chiyo's new friend and Laurie's current addition to their little group, explained. She stopped beside him and gestured at the building. "We're only here to observe, right?"

Kaiden stared at her for a moment, his expression confused before he sighed and pried his helmet off. "I've been here for three years and didn't even realize that was an option."

"Really? Akello demonstrated that during your first Animus test, didn't she?" Chiyo asked.

"Technically, my first time was with Laurie. But I guess I remember that." He placed his helmet to the side and braced himself with his hand as he moved from his crouched position to sit and let his legs dangle over the edge. "I guess it never clicked or I thought it was an advisor option or something."

"To be fair, we don't use it much when we're together," Genos interjected and swept his gaze over the forest. "We engineers use it on occasion when training on new machines or systems. It enables us to get up close and observe before actively trying to dismantle or repair it, so it's quite handy."

"You should keep in mind that this is still only a theoretical layout," Cyra stated, pointed to the building, and traced it in the air with her finger. "The outside is probably fairly accurate. We actually found a few pictures of it, but all interior pictures were from bad angles. They were clearly taken in a hurry and most weren't even labeled yet so we don't know if they were of the same building or multiple ones."

"I don't think it matters that much," Kaiden admitted. "That factory we destroyed was nice and everything but the way it was built...well, it seemed standard."

"It certainly wasn't made for human comfort," Chief agreed as he appeared on Kaiden's shoulder and turned to look at Cyra. "Did y'all find anything in those files about a human side of the operation?"

"No indexes or membership ledgers or anything like that. But the assassin left notes that she was in contact with or saw at least a few dozen people during her tenure with Kaiden's attacker, Dario," she responded. "He didn't happen to mention anything himself, did he?" she asked her companions. "Let something slip, perhaps?"

"Most of it was prattle." Chiyo answered first as she stepped up to them with Genos beside her. "He seemed more interested in gloating or making cheeky remarks." She looked at Kaiden. "But he made some rather cryptic remarks to Kaiden before he got away."

"I have a feeling I should get used to that." He sighed. "Granted, he was an enemy, so it makes more sense. As for what he said, it wasn't much, but he did seem to indicate that the AO was real. Still, I guess with the drive, that's somewhat moot."

Cyra frowned and turned to Chiyo. "Has your father been in touch? Has anything else happened to his company since?"

"Nothing they've been able to find, but they are all on high-alert now, which is probably why they haven't been so bold lately."

A stream of bots poured from the entrance of the building and caught their attention. "This is the first time I'll do real fieldwork in over three years." Cyra chuckled, her gaze locked on the mechanical legion as it continued to march out. "Do you really think this is possible? I don't wanna sound nervous, but…" She shrugged.

"It would probably be more worrisome if you weren't," the other infiltrator assured her and earned an appreciative smile.

"To be honest," Kaiden began and his companions turned to look at him. Chief's bright avatar illuminated his face as the sky darkened quickly above. "I suppose it all comes down to the reinforcements I can get us. We all have our parts to play to prepare, but by my count, we have the four of us, Wolfson, Sasha, and maybe an old friend of mine. As much as I would like to be an optimist here, I don't think a party of seven will do much good—at least with the current plan of destroying the place and living to tell about it."

"I should add that I am all about that plan," Cyra said with a thumbs-up.

"I am partial to it myself," Genos agreed.

"Then I guess I gotta rally the troops." He stood with a small smile at the others. "That's my gig right now."

"Do you have a place to start?" Chiyo asked. "Maybe Julio?"

"I'll talk to him tomorrow after my workshops," he confirmed. "But I had him set up an appointment with someone else. The good news is I think he may go for it, crazy as the situation may be."

"And the bad?" Genos asked.

"Well, all he can do is help me get my foot in the door," he explained as he opened a screen in front of him. "As far as the people I'm looking into are concerned, I would say that the chances of them joining the fight range from good to eh. I honestly hope that I won't have to actually go and talk to one of them."

"Who are you trying to recruit?" Cyra asked.

"First off will be the Fire Riders." He continued to scroll through the screen. "They have several divisions along the west coast and probably have the most reason to want to take a little revenge on the AO, even if they don't really know what's going on."

"And the others?" Chiyo asked as Genos stepped curiously closer to Kaiden.

"The Skyway Kings. I only worked with them once during the Ramses incident, but they seem to have some rapport with the Riders. I hope they'll pitch in, even if it's only in return for helping them back then. But that may be a bust as it wasn't exactly for free."

"You've filled in quite an amount of your soldier tree, friend Kaiden," Genos noted, impressed as he looked the tree on the screen and noted the blocks of white indicating a filled talent.

"Yeah. I have a couple of points left but nothing worthwhile I can use them on at the moment." He sighed and switched to the general tree. "Strategic Mind needs three to progress. I'm only halfway through with it."

"I keep telling you that should have been one of your priority talents," Chief teased.

"You realize I've poured nearly sixty points into you alone, right?" Kaiden retorted.

"Ya can't say it wasn't well spent can, ya?"

"So only those two gangs?" Cyra asked. "Fair enough, I guess gang knowledge isn't my forte, but I don't think they would make for massive armies."

"Massive isn't really want we want," Genos countered. "It'll be risky raiding this place without the military or police force getting suspicious. A smaller group of a few hundred would work better."

"That's small?" The ace looked disappointed. "I actually

thought more on the massive side—maybe a few hundred guys muscled to the gills would be a sufficient force and damn intimidating. I guess I need to rethink my idea of massive."

The Tsuna tapped his infuser. "To be fair, most Tsuna battles are known for having thousands of combatants at once."

"That must be a sight." Kaiden smirked at the thought, then looked at Cyra. "To answer your question, those are the two I feel good about. The third, not so much."

"And who are they?" Chiyo asked.

"The Azure Halos," he responded with a frown.

"The Halos?" She grimaced. "When did you run into them?"

"On the first big mission I did after my run-in with Gin. I'm not sure how well that will go. I don't think they will hate me because I did technically save them from a killer robot. But they lost so many people that the boys I electro-cuted may technically be the bosses now."

"You do seem to have an odd way to meet new people," Cyra commented jokingly after an uncomfortable silence.

"I stole one of their jet-bikes too," he admitted.

"Okay, then. Let's put them on the 'probably not' list." She sighed and stared at the ground for a moment before looking up. "I know you want to confront these guys and after everything the professor told me, I want to be there as well. I was worried you might go in half-cocked but I'm a little more at ease knowing you have a plan going in."

"Trust me, she wouldn't let me otherwise," Kaiden said and nodded at Chiyo, who merely played it off with an innocent smile. "And I guess I'm simply not that brash anymore. Victory doesn't mean much unless you can enjoy it. If anything, I'm worried about the aftermath."

"You are kicking the metaphorical hive," Genos agreed.

"But the way I see it is that they are doing something anyway—something that seems to involve us or the Academy as a whole. If we succeed, we can potentially find something conclusive we can show the world and hobble them at the same time. Kill two birds and all that."

"That sounds logical." Genos propped his chin in his hand and stared off in thought. "I don't seem to know as much about this organization as you do, but they are scheming to go against humanity, right?"

"The way they see it, according to the professor, is that they are scheming for humanity," Cyra explained. "An arbiter is someone whose power and authority is considered absolute—a kind of guiding hand of authority. They think they are doing whatever they do for the benefit of humanity. Or, at least, that was the old rumor when people talked about them."

"Most shadowy collectives of bastards like to think that way." Kaiden sighed. "You see it all the time in terrorist organizations and the like—the can't fix an omelet without breaking a few eggs metaphor. Why do the eggs always have to be genocide or something like that?"

"Many villains see themselves as the heroes in their own story, tragically," Chiyo added, her expression one of distaste.

"The problem is that it isn't only their own story they are writing." Kaiden huffed. "I don't know if it's only world domination they are going for, but they are trying to control things and they have targeted the Academy, at the very least. And for at least another year, that's quite personal." He offered an outstretched hand to his team. "We won't let them have that, will we?"

The three looked down and Genos nodded quickly and placed his hand on Kaiden's. Chiyo and Cyra smiled at each other and added theirs as well.

"This is a little cheesy, but I'm ready to do whatever I can," Cyra promised.

"And we'll all do the same," the ace promised. "And it's a good thing too because we have tons of prep to do."

CHAPTER EIGHT

Jiro sat under one of the massive oak trees in the forest. He tapped his fingers impatiently as he waited for the others to arrive and grew steadily more concerned. The leader's message had been clear to meet at this time and now, it was almost five minutes past. He expected such slovenly actions from Jensen, but Xiulan and Nolan should at least be professional.

"Hello there." A familiar voice spoke into the silence. Jiro's eyes widened when Dario walked casually down the forest path, smiling secretively—which was disconcerting, at the best of times. But more worrisome was the fact that he wore his gauntlets.

"Dear Council Leader."

What was he doing there? Was he the one who had actually sent the message? Was this some sort of coup and were the others in trouble?

Honestly, he was more afraid for himself. The man always had a dangerous edge to him and being alone with him while he had his device—an instrument of death he had used to kill hundreds, if not thousands, of people—left him more than a little agitated. He'd rather not be alone with him without his guards. Still, he hoped it wouldn't come to that. The assassin couldn't be there for him, right? He had been loyal and taken care of all operations given to him. There could be no reason why Merrick wanted him gone, could there?

The grass rustled and sticks snapped behind him. He turned quickly and when Merrick walked into view from behind a group of trees, he didn't feel as safe as he had hoped. The coldness in the organization leader's eyes was chilling, although fortunately, they didn't seem to be looking at him but at Dario.

"Do you really want to do this now, Dario?" Merrick asked and the other man stopped in his tracks and raised his head. His smile widened slightly but his hands remained in his pockets.

"You haven't kept me busy enough," he stated. "Plus, how many times do we have a chance to dance with an audience watching?"

Jiro fell back and stammered, "Wait—excuse me?"

Merrick stopped and turned slowly to finally notice the councilman where he sat, confused, under the tree. "Ah, Jiro, what are you doing here?"

"I-I-I got a m-message, sir!" he stammered and his gaze flicked warily from one to the other.

"That was from me," Dario admitted. "I wanted to gather more but realized you probably wouldn't appreciate getting everyone involved."

The leader gazed at Juro for a little longer before his gaze returned to the other man. "Was this really necessary at all? You shouldn't interrupt others' important work, Dario."

"I thought about sending another message and calling it off. But our dear councilman seemed so tense at the meeting," the assassin responded. He inclined his head toward Jiro and leaned back a little as if to study him. "I felt he could use a good show to relieve his stress and that he might learn something."

"Why me? I do recon and subterfuge and focus on companies. I'm not inclined to combat!" Jiro hissed his outrage before he managed to catch his next words and stood abruptly. "I appreciate the thought, Dario, but I feel it is inappropriate for me to be here. I shall leave you and sir Rayne to handle your own—"

"Don't get all weak in the knees because someone is looking at you with bloodlust in their eyes," Merrick stated and caught the councilman off guard. "I am sorry that my friend has disturbed you. But you should take note. After all, with the way things are proceeding, you may not have a choice when the invasion starts."

Jiro was silent. Not have a choice? What was he insinuating? At a rustle behind Dario, both Merrick and his assistant looked in that direction with confusion. The assassin finally drew his hands out of his pockets and the gauntlets began to line up. Jiro noticed that both men were on edge and realized that neither knew who was approaching. Sweat beaded on his brow despite his sudden chill and he slid a shaking hand under his coat to retrieve his pistol.

"Man, these woods are dense," a large man bellowed as he shoved several branches out of his way. Jiro didn't know him, but Dario lowered his arms and sighed, unperturbed by the new invaders.

"Lycan, was it?" the assassin asked as he strolled over to the man, who scratched the side of his head vigorously to dislodge some of the leaves from his hair. "What are you doing here? I don't think I've ever seen one of you without the others."

"We are a rather close group, sir." A tanned man with an easy smile walked into view from behind his larger friend. "Sorry to bother you."

"Jalloh," Dario said to acknowledge the leader while Raz, the hacker, and their sniper, Cascina, also appeared. "Good to see you." He released a group of nanos that immediately formed into an explosive orb. Jalloh dodged it easily and Raz simply stepped forward and grabbed it. The amber light within faded while Lycan and Cascina watched the assassin warily. She made her caution far more obvious, however, when she drew her rifle and aimed it at him.

"I like your enthusiasm," Dario mused when he noted Raz tapping the air with a gloved hand—obviously a way to hack into his nanos—and the sniper ready to fire. Casually, he waved an arm and the orb activated in Raz's hand, who quickly released it and jumped back. He chuckled as he brought the orb back to him and disassembled it to return the nanos to their containers. "Forgive me. I'm a little excitable right now."

"I know the feeling." Lycan chuckled and pounded a fist into his other hand.

The assassin looked at Jalloh. "How can I help you?"

The man leaned against a nearby tree. "I'm sorry to

bother you, but we have a complaint about the man you left us with."

"Nolan?" Dario asked with a hasty glance at Merrick and Jiro before he gave them a reassuring wave. "Is he working you too hard?"

"Oh, that's certainly not the problem," Lycan muttered. "It's more like he isn't working us at all. We've sat in three different factories simply twiddling our thumbs."

"As much as it seems we may be shooting ourselves in the foot," Raz stated, his voice modulated in his mask, "given that we're essentially being paid to kick around, we're rather bored."

"I'm sure you can relate as a fellow assassin," Jalloh added.

Dario ran a hand through his hair. "Nolan is something of a worrywart, I must admit. He's readying for a war, which makes one a little scattershot."

"That's why we wanted to talk," the merc leader stated. "We're all good going to war and even took part in a couple on the stations. But if we won't do anything until then, we'd prefer to come back to your employ. You are still the one paying us, after all."

"I suppose that's right, although I guess I should have had the organization pay the expenses. But as it stands, I'm having problems with that myself." Dario glanced at Merrick and gestured to the group. "Would you care to step in, *capo*?"

Jiro wanted to throttle the man for his disrespect, but Merrick merely sighed and approached to address the mercenary team. "My apologies that you haven't found your current work satisfying." He glanced meaningfully at

Dario as he said that. "As of right now, I will take over your orders. Don't worry about the general."

"No complaints here, boss!" Lycan yelled as he shook the leader's hand enthusiastically and almost caused Jiro's skull to erupt with outrage and indignation. "What do you have for us?"

"One last trip," he answered. "I need you to observe one of our strongholds. You'll be outfitted with experimental equipment while there."

"More babysitting?" Lycan muttered and his head tilted in disapproval and suspicion.

"Oh no, I need your expertise for practical purposes," he assured them. "This is a very important facility. It can't be as easily hidden as the others, however. We've noticed people snooping around and we need you to take care of them."

"At least that's something," Raz muttered and Cascina nodded silently.

"I would prefer you do it discreetly, but I know how demanding that kind of order can be." He cast another glance at Dario, who merely chuckled. "So, if it does get rough, please dispose of the evidence."

"Not a problem," Lycan declared.

"Is there anything else we should know or look for?" Jalloh asked.

"I have people there who can fill you in and keep you busy, if nothing else, to test the latest droids." Merrick noticed a small frown on Lycan's face. "Don't worry. They will easily satiate any residual bloodlust you may have."

"Is that right?" The large man stroked his chin thoughtfully. "Well, I'll hold you to that. When can we leave?"

"Immediately." The AO leader clapped Dario on the back. "Assuming my friend here can get everything in order."

"So I'm a secretary now, *capo*?" the man snarked and threw his hands up. "Fine. I'll get it done, but I hope you'll have something for me when I get back."

"I have a few ideas, do not worry," he promised and tapped the top of his cane. "I would prefer you to do good for the organization rather than the alternative."

"You wound me," Dario said melodramatically and rested his hand over his heart before he spun and placed a hand on Jalloh's shoulder. "Very well, let's get you doing something fun for a while, shall we?"

They walked away and Merrick watched them for a moment before he spoke to Jiro. "I'm sorry you had to deal with all that, Jiro," he stated and smiled benignly. "But I hope you took something from it, even a little. You're free to go. Please take care of your orders."

"Yes, sir, of course." He nodded. The leader did the same and walked away into the forest. Jiro looked at his trembling hands, grasped one with the other, and gritted his teeth. He would possibly have to enter battle? He balled one fist and tried to stop the shaking as he looked around the forest. It appeared desolate but filled with color and beauty. Oddly enough, he recalled, he'd had the same feeling when he first met Merrick.

Battle. If his leader called him to do it, he would.

CHAPTER NINE

Genos looked a little dubiously at the colorful liquid in his cup, which contained very little alcohol overall but a considerable amount of the sweet syrup. He felt a little nauseous and recalled the last time he imbibed too much.

"You don't have to drink it, you know," Kaiden pointed out and finished his beer. "I simply thought you would want something while we waited."

"No, no, thank you, friend Kaiden." He took the glass and swirled the contents for a moment before he took a small sip and set it down again. "It's quite good."

"You know, I've seen you charge into a horde of killer droids with less hesitation," the ace stated with amusement and leaned back in his chair. "And yet your weakness is sugar water."

"Maybe it would be better if I introduced it into my infuser," Genos muttered. He moved a hand to a small port on the side of the machine around his neck but hesitated. "No. I'd better not."

"Yeah. I still don't really know how your biology works, but you might not want to introduce alcohol and dye into the thing that helps you breathe." He chuckled.

"Do you need a refill, Kaiden?" Julio asked and sidled over with another glass.

"Would you kindly?" He looked at the door while the proprietor removed his empty glass. "He should be here soon, yeah?"

"He should be, but I haven't seen him except for one other time since the Ramses gig," he stated and followed the ace's gaze to the entrance. "I'm honestly not sure what to make of him. Guys like that are usually timely as a rule. They are technically the first impression of any company they work for."

"Gang, in this case," Genos noted.

Kaiden nodded, sipped his beer, and caught Julio's arm before he left. "I'll pay for his drinks, so give him whatever."

"No problem. I'll give you fair warning, though. He doesn't usually order the expensive stuff, but he orders a good few rounds of the mid-tier."

"It should be fine. Hopefully, I won't have too many expenditures if everything goes right." He grinned at the barkeep. "Other than the rental fee on your baby."

"You're paying for quality, you know," Julio stated and smiled at Genos. "It was a smart move to bring him along. You took care of that ship beautifully. There was hardly any dust after the explosion."

"You knew about that?" the Tsuna asked.

"Of course. I watched the cameras after you came back." He laughed as he returned to the main bar.

"He was probably making sure I didn't secretly screw something up," Kaiden muttered and checked his tablet. "He trusts me to take care of a gang leader or for recon on rival businesses but doesn't trust me with his toys."

"His ship is a toy?" Genos questioned. "He seems to have expensive hobbies."

Kaiden chuckled but it faded when he saw no messages from Sasha. He sighed as he placed his tablet in his backpack. Both he and Genos looked up in surprise when a man with tanned skin and disheveled hair slouched into the seat opposite them.

"Uh, can I help you?" the ace asked.

The man smiled. "I hope so since I was told you were looking for me."

He studied him curiously and finally, recognition dawned. "Rok? Holy hell, you look different."

"Yeah. I've been running my happy ass back and forth from California to here so haven't had much time for personal grooming." The Fire Rider recruiter caught a passing waitress by the hand and asked for a scotch before he turned back to them. "So, what do ya need, my friend?"

"Straight to business, then?" Kaiden leaned back. The man looked far more haggard than he had at their first meeting, but he seemed calmer as well. Granted, the fact that he wasn't looking for help for a situation that was going tits-up at that moment was probably helpful. Or maybe he was simply better at hiding it now.

"Like I said, I've been on the trail. The Riders have had consistent work in Cali so need more bodies. I'm one of the best they have, and unfortunately, they seem to know that." He chuckled, retrieved an opened pack of Sinner's

Blend cigarettes, and lit one. "I can't complain too much, though. The commission adds up to a rather pretty cred."

"Hello again, Rok." Julio greeted him, handed him his scotch, and sat quickly. "I don't see you around here too often—not the greatest recruiting place?"

"Hey, it's the big man himself." Rok chuckled, picked the glass up, and toasted him. "Julio, right? Nah, you have nice clientele, but that's kind of the problem when you're looking for guys who are willing to take on the gang life." He turned and toasted Kaiden. "I guess I got lucky with you and your friends, huh?"

"I guess so." He shrugged. "Hopefully, a little of that luck rubs off on me."

"Is that so?" The gang recruiter took a sip and smiled at the taste. "I guess I'll go back to my first question, then. What do ya need? It's been a while since we talked. I assumed it must be something interesting for you to drop a line out of the blue."

"Interesting? I guess so, but that's something of a long story," Kaiden admitted and lifted his glass. "The long and short of it is that I need men—which you seem to have in good supply."

"Oh, the Riders have plenty now." He nodded. "There's even of talk of turning into a proper merc company. But you know that won't come without incentive for them." He leaned forward and looked directly into the ace's eyes. "I'm not really the guy you talk to for that, but it shouldn't be too much trouble to get you in talks. Before I stick my neck out, though, I have to know what you plan to do with all these guys you're looking for."

"We intend to destroy a stronghold owned and operated by a group that is trying to take over the world," Kaiden stated flatly. Rok raised an eyebrow in surprise. "You may or may not believe that, but it'll be a raid, either way. I'm sure I don't have the credits to hire a large force, but what I do have—or rather they have—is a huge amount of new and shiny tech that these men are more than welcome to take for themselves."

"Are you okay with that?" the man inquired. "Or, rather, whoever you're working for is?"

"I'm not working for anyone. This is my mission," he stated flatly. "In fact, this may push even the grey boundaries of merc work."

"Getting truly dirty, huh? That's not really gonna be an issue for the Fire Riders," Rok admitted. "That promise of tech will probably be enough for you to muster a small army out of interest, but I imagine this won't be an easy raid."

"Personally, I don't think easy is ever an option in a raid," Julio pointed out.

"You'd be surprised what a lot of hollering and a few gunshots can accomplish." The other man chuckled and took another sip. "So, this super-villain group—who are they exactly?"

"I can't give you all the details, mostly because we're still finding out ourselves," Kaiden said. "But we do know, thanks to some info we recovered, that they were the ones who hired the EX-10 to attack Ramses."

"Really now?" Rok leaned back, set his drink down, and tilted his head in thought. "That would be a group the Riders would want to take on, and maybe even the Kings. I can't really speak for them, though."

"That's my hope as well," the ace replied. "And something else you might want to know is that they are probably the ones that brought Gin Sonny to Earth."

The man sucked in a breath and the hand holding the glass tightened. "Gin...the one who killed Lazar?"

"Yeah, his friends as well," he confirmed.

Rok was silent. The jovial atmosphere he had brought seemed to cool and he looked at the table for a moment before he stood. "I'll be back," he said and moved quickly away to a quiet side of the bar.

"That seemed to shake him," Julio commented.

"It did something." Kaiden agreed. "When I spoke to him about Lazar last time, he seemed to have made some kind of peace with it already, but I guess he was a heavier loss than I thought."

"You should know that certain guys will always leave an impression, especially in a gang," the man reminded him. "You can make peace with a death but never really move on."

"At least not until you have a chance to avenge them."

The proprietor nodded and pushed his chair back. "It's a dangerous line of thinking but certainly true."

"Are you heading back?" Kaiden asked as he finished his second beer.

"Yeah. I'm too busy to idle around," he admitted. "I came to act as a middleman if necessary, but it looks like you've got this."

"This is only the first part. I still have to talk to someone in charge, and I don't know when that will be."

"Can you leave tonight?" Rok asked and appeared at the table.

"Tonight?"

"I have someone—two people, actually. They do have a mission prepared but still have time to pull out if you can make a better offer," the man stated. "But you have to meet tonight."

"Where?"

"San Diego. You'll meet Zena and Desmond again." The recruiter entered something into his tablet. "I'm sending you the location. Be there around eight if you can."

Kaiden nodded, stood quickly, and looked at Genos. "It's after four now. Can you go with me?"

"Of course, friend Kaiden." The Tsuna nodded and pushed his not even half-finished drink aside.

"Julio!" the ace called. "Can we get the—"

"I already sent Genos the codes," the man responded. "It's yours, kid. Come back before the big day. I'll have something else ready for ya."

He nodded and shouted his thanks as he and Genos hurried out. Rok and Julio watched them leave. The recruiter thought of the opportunity for the Riders to get their vengeance, and Julio thought of the man who had set up the gig in the Amazon that almost left Kaiden dead.

Both hoped that this would end with payback.

CHAPTER TEN

Kaiden stood and peered out of the cockpit as Genos piloted the dropship over the location Rok had given them. Only one building with functioning lights was visible, surrounded by dark streets and ramshackle huts and shelters that dotted the area.

"Is this one of their main bases?" he questioned, more thinking aloud than asking his companion. "Rok said they wanted to possibly turn into a mercenary company, right? I know most people who need a group of mercs won't exactly look for hot towels and glacial water at reception, but I don't think this will impress very many."

"It is likely that this is some kind of safe haven or relatively secret location," Genos suggested as he circled the vessel in search of a landing area. "I may not be familiar with this group, but with how hastily this was put together, they probably feel safer discussing terms with us here rather than in a more open and busy area."

He frowned and sat again. "That's a good point. Rok said I was talking to Zena and Desmond. Unless something has changed in the months since Ramses, they are only captains of their local chapters. This might be a private matter—one they don't want to bring up to the gangs as a whole."

"Can you think of a reason?" his companion asked. "That recruiter seemed to be rather despondent when you mentioned Lazar's death. I would imagine that the incident affected others. These Fire Riders extend all the way to the Midwest, correct? I would think many more wish for their own piece of justice."

"You have the right idea, but as Julio hinted, guys like that can make a strong impact on gangs. For guys who are taken into the fold early, they can be like family," he explained and his eyes closed for a moment. "But it's like a family and a company in one, and some only want to move their way up the ladder. I remember Lazar saying something about trying to bring change to the Riders and not everyone was happy about that. It makes me wonder where Zena falls on the map."

"What about the other leader?" Genos asked. He finally found a place to set the ship down and began to descend slowly. "He's not part of the Riders, correct?"

Kaiden shook his head. "No, he leads a chapter of the Skyway Kings. Those guys were unique for the fact that they were one of the few gangs that used aerial tactics with gliders, Zepps, jetpacks, and the like. It kind of came back to bite them after a while since their ground forces weren't as competent for a time. From what I saw at Ramses, it seems they righted that, for the most part." He looked at Genos as the vessel finally set down. "I honestly don't know much about them. That was the only time I really interacted with them. I should probably let you know that I don't know how this will turn out."

The Tsuna unlatched his belt. "Do you think this will be a trap?"

"It's hard to say," he admitted as he released his own belt and stood. "I would say that it isn't. I don't see a reason why they would want to hurt us and there isn't a grudge. Admittedly, we left them to deal with any fallout after we took care of the EX-10, but that was merely the business of being mercs in that situation. They had more leeway as 'hired' security for the company."

"I wasn't there, obviously, but considering that Rok seemed pleasant around you, I don't think he would try to lead you to danger." Genos put his helmet on as they entered the bay together.

Kaiden picked up Debonair, folded the grip against the barrel, and placed it into a compartment on the underside of his gauntlet. His blade was in the same position on the opposite arm and both allowed for quick access to them should he need it. "I don't think so either but unfortunately, too many people are really good at keeping their intentions hidden." He snickered as he pressed the button to open the side door. "I also might be good at psyching myself out at the worst times."

"I see." The Tsuna paused to check his gauntlet. When he clenched his fist and pumped it, electrodes protruded from the knuckles and sparked. He repeated the motion and they collapsed. "If you are, it's because you are being cautious."

"Do you think so?" he muttered as he turned to close the door behind them.

"I do, and I think it is good. You worry for the sake of the safety of others," Genos explained as the two began to stride down the hill into the empty town and toward the lit building. "We may be different lifeforms, but I think that is a universal mindset for a leader."

"I'm glad I can live up to it." He released a deep sigh. "It's kind of stressful, though."

His companion chuckled beside him and nodded. "That is also universal, I think."

The two friends pushed the doors to the building open and immediately encountered a couple of dozen gang members who stared at them. There seemed to be more members in the red and orange reminiscent of fire for the Riders but a few wore the sky-blue colors of the Kings as well.

Kaiden paused and looked around. "Are your captains around?" he asked when no one seemed inclined to speak to them.

"You're punctual. I like that." Desmond's voice rang out and he strode down a flight of stairs dressed in a dark shirt —a little too tight for his large frame—and dark blue pants. He reached the foot of the stairs and leaned against the railing. "I wish you had been as punctual at Ramses."

The ace raised his hands and shrugged. "You can't really put that on me. We were shot out of the sky before we even reached the location."

"And yet you still made it anyway," the man recalled. "I don't think I ever had the chance to thank you and your friends properly. You made a hell of a difference back then." His gaze drifted to Genos and focused on the infuser barely visible around the neck of his helmet. "Wait, speak of the devil—is that Jaxon?"

Kaiden shook his head and thumbed at Genos as he opened his mouth to respond, but the Tsuna stepped forward. "I am his kin, Genos Aronnax, I apologize that I could not join both you and him on that night, I was… dealing with some unpleasantness."

"Kin, huh? As in sibling or cousin?" Desmond asked.

"A little of both but also not really," Kaiden summarized with little clarity. "To be honest, their whole clan system still confuses me."

The gang captain laughed. "Well, either way, your kin is a hell of a fighter. I owe him one too."

"Is Zena here?"

The Skyway Kings leader nodded and pointed up the stairs. "Yeah, she's helping with inventory. Did Rok tell you we are preparing to go on another mission?"

"Yeah, but you were still willing to hear me out. Thanks for sparing the time."

He raised a hand casually. "No problem. Like I said, we owed you one."

A quick glance at the various members of the gangs confirmed that while some talked amongst themselves, others continued to stare at the visitors. "I thought the Ramses mission was a one-time thing. Do you and the Riders work together regularly?"

"On the big jobs yeah," Desmond replied. "We don't have much back up here. Most of the Fire Riders are based in the Midwest and the Kings on the East Coast. Hell, I don't think we would have a chapter here if it weren't for some member getting a wild hair up his ass a few decades ago and deciding to start a chapter because he thought it would 'expand influence.'" He made air quotes to finish his statement. "I wonder if the big chapters even officially recognize us. We hardly use the aerial gear the Kings are known for. We have a few real ballbusters in our group but unfortunately, we have three times as many who only think they are badasses when they are actually dumba—"

At a crash in a room off to the left, Desmond stiffened and turned. "Dammit, Kars, I swear to Christ if you broke another jetpack, I'll jam a Zeppelin down your throat and activate it!"

Kaiden snickered along with several other members. Another set of footsteps on the stairs announced Zena, who sauntered down dressed in an orange top that matched her hololenses and white pants. "Kaiden, it's good to see you again." She greeted him with a grin.

"Same here, Zena," he replied as he shook her hand. "I left kind of in a hurry. What did Rok tell you?"

"Not much, only that you wanted to talk about a job. What had me interested was how he said it," she admitted and folded her arms as Desmond returned from where he'd gone to check on his clumsy teammates and now joined them again. "He was serious and almost grim. Whatever you talked about seems to have shaken him."

"That wasn't my intention." He sighed. "I told him I have a job that requires a large team of guys. It's basically a raid on what is best described as a fortress, even though the details still need to be worked out."

"What kind of raid?" the other man asked. "And against who?"

"Kind?" The ace considered that carefully. "Honestly, I'm fine with total destruction."

"Damn," one of the gang members muttered and Zena quieted them with a sharp glance.

"As for who, that's kind of tricky. But let's go with a mutual enemy."

"Mutual how?" she asked.

Kaiden retrieved his tablet. "Well, for one thing, they were the ones who sic'd EX-10 on Ramses," he revealed and showed a document on the tablet to the two leaders. "That's something for both of you. But for the Riders, they also brought the killer Gin Sonny to Earth, who killed Lazar."

Zena pursed her lips, her expression cold. "Is that right? I wish I could take a shot at him still, but I suppose I could settle for them."

"I did not know him myself," Genos stated and placed a hand on his chest. "But from Rok's reaction and yours, I can tell he is missed. My condolences."

"Thanks, but we prefer action if someone hurts one of our own," she stated and her eyes looked over her lenses at the members around her. "But, as much as I would like to accept on only the grounds of causing these guys a little misery, I have to think about all my guys. I'm sure most who were at Ramses want some revenge for those lost, but we've had a fairly large number of new recruits and transfers in the months since and need to build our stocks up. Unless you have the creds to match our current gig, I'm gonna have to decline for now."

"Same here." Desmond sighed and handed the tablet back.

"I'm almost certain I can't match it in credits," Kaiden admitted and opened a new file on the tablet. "But I can maybe balance that in loot."

"You wanna raid a pirate fortress or something?" the other man joked.

"The place I want to attack is full of new tech, expensive materials, weapons, armor, the works." He flipped the tablet around to display a number of pictures as proof. "We're only interested in data—info about this group—so you can have anything you can carry with you."

Zena and Desmond scanned the images. He definitely had an excited smile and while Zena was more neutral, she gave a nod of approval. "It's more of a pain than getting paid upfront, but if it has a haul like this, we could not only re-outfit but sell the extras."

"We'd get way more credits that way too. Hell, we'd probably use most of the credits we'd get from this job to get weapons and all that, but probably ones that aren't as good as these." The gang leader glanced at the woman and took another look at the pictures. "I can't even figure out what some of them are."

"Some seem to be modified or updated models of Sovereign guns," Kaiden said and indicated two images specifically. "Others seem to be handmade, something you won't find on the market."

"Not even the black market," Zena agreed as she studied the remaining pictures. "What do you think this will cost us? In mortal terms."

"That all depends on your boys and girls," the ace replied and gestured behind him. "I have some elites joining us and maybe some high-level weapons available, but they seem to have a mostly droid force, and they've been building it up for some time. It'll all be down to how much damage we can do and how quickly."

"Pure brute force?" Desmond asked.

"I have…a couple of hackers," he replied. "They can probably help out but that'll take time to set up. Until they can get into the systems, brute force will probably be the majority of the battle."

Zena and Desmond looked at each other. "Between the two of us, we have a little over two-hundred members we can call in," she revealed. "We can certainly provide arms and power, but that'll wear out against a droid onslaught after too long."

"I'm sure we have a few who dabble in hacking. But most work in cracking, which isn't really practical on a large scale," her gang comrade noted.

Kaiden nodded and wished he had brought Chiyo. She might have had a better understanding of what cracking versus hacking might add to their advantage. "Yeah. My guess is that this fight will be won or lost in a day. We don't really want to hold out that long, even if we can. They would probably simply call in reinforcements. We aren't really trying to destroy them completely—although it would be a pleasure if we could—but rather to send a message."

"We'll try to stall the guys who gave us our current gig," Zena promised, added her number into the tablet's directory, and handed it to him. "We're interested, but I would like a little reassurance that we actually have a chance to stop the droids rather than simply whittle them down while others are built."

Desmond nodded. "I have some contacts who could possibly help. But they don't run very cheap."

"It's fine." The ace stowed the tablet carefully. "I have an idea of my own."

"Really? It sounds like you've thought ahead." The other man sounded enthusiastic.

Zena tilted her head and regarded him warily. "You don't look that confident or excited, though."

Kaiden threw his hands up and spun to head to the doors. Genos hurried to catch up. "Unlike you, I'm not so sure these guys will be excited to help—or even to see me."

"Do you need help?" Desmond asked. "You're right—I'm actually excited about this raid. If you need help—"

"It's okay." He waved to stop a possible protest. "It would probably only make it worse, actually. The Halos like to keep to themselves."

Zena and Desmond looked at each other in surprise. "The Azure Halos?" he asked in a strangled tone.

CHAPTER ELEVEN

Chiyo held back the feelings of nausea and pain. She focused on the lights, numbers, and commands around her and they gradually grounded her. In today's training, she'd managed eleven minutes but could go longer. Cyra, who casually adjusted a literal data stream, floated in a swirling mass of lights. The student infiltrator should have been able to see what her colleague was writing. The experience shouldn't be so intense.

"Are you all right, Chi?" the woman asked in concern when she realized her companion was under strain.

"I should be..." She sighed and drew another slow breath. "This is...much more intense than I thought it would be."

"I'm surprised." Cyra floated to her and place a hand on her shoulder. "When we interfaced with the Animus system last year and tried to help Kaiden, you seemed so calm. Up until the very end, too, like it didn't affect you at all."

"I think Chief helped with that at the time," she

explained and changed her position from cross-legged to lean back and drift rather than hover. "When I use the technician suite, it's usually only to transfer control and move the device like it is my own body."

"That only works on certain machines, I'm afraid," the other woman reasoned and floated along with her fellow hacker. "For the complicated stuff, we have to be able to interact with it directly—let our minds form something more tangible and believable so we can manipulate it personally."

Chiyo tried to adjust her responses based on what her colleague had said. Modernist cubes of varying sizes representing functions or files filled the area and littered what could be considered the ground. The glowing streams of data in various colors were occasionally interspersed with orbs that indicated security programs. She returned her focus to her companion. "This is what our minds consider believable?"

Cyra giggled. "More believe than merely a landscape of binary. We may be smart but we're not quantum computers."

"It looks fascinating…" She made another study of their surroundings and located the horizon as it ebbed between white and a light-blue color. "I assume this is because our EIs are trying to make it simple so as to not use too much power."

"One of the reasons is that they are focused on making sure our minds don't melt away."

"That would be an issue." Chiyo straightened when she thought she felt a dull pain nudging at her mind. "Fourteen minutes. I'll make it to twenty."

"Don't strain yourself," the woman warned. "That fact that you made it to ten is already incredible. I wasn't able to do that until a few years after I left the Academy."

"We need every advantage we can have," she reasoned and spun to face her. "Even if we are able to stop the droids, there are internal defenses and back-up systems. Not only that, we want to be able to find as much information as we can before Kaiden does what he inevitably does."

Cyra chuckled. "Can't rein in your boyfriend yet?"

"Boy—" she whispered before she simply smiled. "I don't wish to. I think playing it safe would only make it more likely for him to mess up."

"Fair point."

A bright flash between them startled both infiltrators, who immediately tensed. A female figure appeared and her body rippled through several shades. *"Good morning, technicians."*

"Aurora?" Cyra lowered her arms that she had used to shield her eyes. "Is the professor looking for me?"

Laurie's EI nodded. *"Both of you, in fact."*

Chiyo frowned. "Can't you simply inform us? I wish to finish my current training."

Aurora smiled. *"You are quite diligent, miss Chiyo, but to show you the files he wishes to share would disrupt the current connection rather drastically. I can appear here with little problem as I interface with your EIs directly and am therefore not seen as a 'new' item. Should I try to link with a whole new system while you are still here... Well, I understand it can be quite painful for those using the technician's suite when sudden changes occur from outside the system."*

"It's not really a headache you can take care of with some aspirin," Cyra confirmed.

Chiyo sighed but nodded. "We'll be there soon," she promised. Laurie's EI nodded and vanished. The infiltrator took a deep breath and glanced at her companion, who nodded and closed her eyes. She did so as well, and when she opened them, she was back in the Animus pod.

"Good morning, ladies," Laurie greeted cheerfully as the two women entered his office.

"Good morning, Professor," Chiyo responded. "Aurora notified us about some new information you wish to pass along."

He nodded. "Well, I suppose it's not exactly 'new.' More like confirmed. She was able to finally break into several locked files that we had a hell of a time opening."

"The assassin was able to use security you had difficulty circumventing?" she inquired, obviously surprised.

"We don't think it was her," Cyra interjected. "We think that among everything she personally recorded and wrote down, she was able to steal a few files here and there but never had a chance to open them."

"Honestly, I would be shocked if she could," the professor stated. "It's a rather devious little system often called the Enigma Spiral. It locks certain passways when—"

"I am familiar with the system, Professor," Chiyo interrupted and caught herself quickly. "I'm sorry. I still feel a little...ill from the interfacing."

He smirked. "I can certainly understand. I really want

to make a breakthrough with that, but neurobiology is not one of my strong suits. Artificial minds are much more fascinating to me—and not as big a problem when they break."

"Within reason," Cyra muttered. She placed a hand on her hip and looked at the professor. "What did you want to inform us about, sir?"

Laurie placed an EI pad on the table and turned it to display a hologram of a large, square building surrounded by what seemed to be a garrison with a few dozen smaller buildings and storage units. "We're still sifting through everything, but we may have a better understanding of the fortress Kaiden wishes to attack," he revealed and pointed to the main building. "It appears similar to the factory you infiltrated a few months back. This one seems to be designed for autonomous creation, for the most part, but we did find a file with a few dozen names so there may be some kind of overseer group."

"It's built like a high-end military outpost," Chiyo noted.

"Probably so it can blend in better and raise less suspicion," the other woman reasoned.

He used two fingers to drag the hologram in one direction to create another image, although this one seemed smaller than the other and didn't have some of the additions the previous one did. "From the looks of things, it very much is a military outpost, albeit one that was written off several decades ago and bought by a private-sector corporation."

"Private sector?" Chiyo questioned. "Does that mean we can trace the AO from the buyer?"

"Potentially, but that's its own hurdle," he admitted. "I'm sure the AO has innumerable proxy businesses and shell companies. Even if the one that bought it is active, they may merely be puppets. I'm sure there's something we can discover but without proper sanction, our search would more likely be criminal activity than a proper investigation. Anything we found would be dismissed in a court."

Cyra frowned. "So what does that mean for the mission? Are we risking our lives for nothing?"

Laurie shook his head. "Oh no. I certainly wouldn't even allow you to go if that was the case. That's a worry for the company itself. As for this doomsday storage box here..." He pointed at the fortress. "I can certainly assure you that what they are building is certainly not legal, and this is technically already in the grey area of mercenary work. Anything you find in there will be free game."

"Which means that whoever is running it has all the more reason to make sure we don't leave," Chiyo added.

His face contorted into an expression somewhere between dark amusement and sadness. "I think that was already well established, by this point."

Cyra looked at Chiyo, who now stared at the floor, her hand pressed against her mouth as thoughts raced through her mind. She finally looked at the professor. "Have you had a chance to tell Kaiden?"

"I tried—first thing when the files were cracked," he confirmed and leaned back in his chair. "I can't get hold of him. My messages are going through but he's not answering."

"That's kind of odd." His assistant folded her arms. "Do you think he's in danger, Chiyo?"

"I hope not," she replied quietly. "But I think it's more likely he's in discussions right now and needs to focus."

"Friend Kaiden, I fear we may crash," Genos warned calmly and alerted the ace, who currently stumbled around the bay.

"These guys have become awfully trigger-happy since last I saw them," he roared when he finally snagged a railing above and managed to steady himself. "Pull up. Genos. I don't think we'll be able to make a safe landing."

"I've come to that conclusion as well." The pilot pulled on the throttle and hastily returned the vessel to a safe altitude. "Fortunately, we weren't in range of their cannons."

"Cannons? They have cannons now?" Kaiden asked, rather surprised. "They've made some upgrades."

"I doubt this will make you abort," the Tsuna said as he banked the ship to turn and gain a little distance from the droids below. "So I certainly hope you have a reasonable alternative?"

"Alternative? Sure. Reasonable? Maybe not, but practical, at least."

"That is more than I could hope for and less than what I wished." The ace sat in the co-pilot's seat and began working on one of the screens. "What are you doing?"

"Looking for the access to— Ah-ha! I found the pod." He pressed a few more buttons and switches. "Chief, gain control of the auto-pilot and keep the ship on low energy consumption. I hope this doesn't take too long, but you never know."

"On it," he acknowledged. *"But you do know there's only one pod, right?"*

"It should be big enough," he reasoned, glanced at his companion, and smiled. "Hey, Genos, wanna cuddle?"

His friend blinked in absolute silence, then stared at him. "I'm...um, not sure. But I think I don't."

He rolled his eyes and caught the Tsuna by the back of his armor. "Too bad. Suit up and get ready for an invasion of personal space."

CHAPTER TWELVE

The teammates kicked against the door of their pod. It took several hard blows before the door was aligned and slid open. They crawled out—although Genos flopped rather than scrambled—and Kaiden stretched his neck and left shoulder with a grimace as he squinted to where the dropship flew away from their destination. "Make sure it doesn't get too far away in case we have to make a quick getaway."

"It's not really like you to be so worried," Chief commented. *"Last time you were here, you acted like a bastard to those Halo guys. Now, it's come back to bite you, huh?"*

"To be fair, I didn't think I would ever come back," he admitted and grinned at Genos, who patted himself to confirm he was in good order and checked his cannon. "Are you okay there, Genos?"

"Better now. That was...claustrophobic," his friend confessed and tapped his visor. "It appears that the enemy that fired on us is now approaching somewhat rapidly. Should we run or fight?"

"How about a little of both?" he suggested and drew Sire. "Let's split up. The force will be about a dozen for each of us assuming they break off evenly. We're on an open plain, so there won't be much to trip over, and as long as we keep our distance, they won't be able to surround us while we pick them off."

"You don't think they will send reinforcements?" Genos inquired.

"It's possible but hopefully, they'll have seen the ship fly off and assume we left. Still, these guys are techies so I'm sure they've picked up some signal of ours."

The Tsuna primed his cannon. "I think destroying a squad of their mechanicals will make negotiations a little harder."

"They gonna be impossible if we can't even get to the front door," he retorted.

His teammate nodded as he ascended the hill. "That's a good point."

Kaiden followed and studied a large group of Assault and Soldier droids—most created from mismatched parts —that clanked steadily toward them. He raised his rifle and peered through the scope. "It looks like they already have reinforcements. I count more than forty now."

"They really don't seem to want visitors." Genos held the trigger of his cannon down. "It looks like we're gonna have to be rather persistent."

"Agreed." He positioned Sire and held the trigger down to collect energy. They fired almost simultaneously when the droids were close enough to aim and their barrage struck the front line to destroy several and force a few back. Kaiden almost laughed when one of the more shoddy droids simply keeled over when a leg shattered. The teammates looked at one another and nodded. Genos broke left while Kaiden went right and they fired into the horde to get their attention. The advancing army separated and followed both parties.

The ace fired his weapon into a group of mechanicals. His shot tore through the chest of one and annihilated another behind it.

"I'm finally getting some endorphins pumping!" He cheered, charged another shot quickly, and fired again. This attack destroyed four droids at once but a few plasma shots narrowly missed his head.

"Make sure to keep the blood inside. It's hard for the endorphins to revel without it," Chief snarked.

"Right," Kaiden acknowledged, released another two rounds, and sprinted through the valley. When he noticed a large stone, he made his way hastily to it, retrieved a thermal, and lobbed it behind him while he ducked into temporary cover. He vented his rifle. "Chief, how many left?"

"I have ten signatures left but can't tell the state they're in, though. Some might only have half a body considering they aren't in the best of shape."

"The Halos must have scraped together whatever they could. It wouldn't surprise me if they've had to deal with police or other gangs trying to destroy them after that problem with the super-droid." He shut the vent on his rifle as lasers began to punch through the rock above him. Cautiously, he circled and fired several shots, which eliminated three more droids. Chief's assessment was almost spot on. Of the droids remaining, only two seemed to actually be anything close to a threat and he almost felt bad when he fired on them and simply tossed another thermal into the area where the rest tried to claw or hobble their way closer. They shattered from the blast, removing the last possible threat.

"That was kind of anti-climactic." Kaiden sighed and vented his rifle again as he wandered the battlefield to examine some of the remaining parts. Honestly, he was a little impressed that they could make functioning droids out of what most people would consider scrap. At the same time, this certainly wasn't the high-tech material and equipment the Halos were known to use and what made them such a powerhouse that even top companies tried to court members.

His comms activated with a small buzz as. "Kaiden, how do you fare?" Genos asked.

He straightened and chuckled. "Honestly, I'm wondering if that's a joke. These droids are more like scarecrows to shoo away squatters and hikers than a real threat."

"I think the same. They did a fairly good job of scuffing the ship, but maybe that was because they could shoot directly into the underside."

"I'm sure they have some fancy mods or maybe good programming. The Halos have done well with a little," he admitted as he kicked a half-exploded head. "Are you almost done? We can meet at the entrance to the junker town."

"I should be…going to…" The Tsuna's voice faded and static filled their comm link.

"Genos?" Kaiden asked and frowned as he wondered what was wrong. He was about to speak again when the ground shifted beneath him. He retreated hastily as the earth opened and clicks and snaps issued from within the chasm. A rush of air seemed to almost hiss at him and something peered over the edge of the yawning hole before it stood slowly to tower several feet above him. His eyes widened and mouth gaped as he stared at a large machine on four legs with a spherical body and what appeared to be two turrets above and a large cannon below.

"Genos, I'll have to call you back," he muttered reflexively, forgetting that his teammate might not actually hear him.

The machine activated and lights coursed over its frame as it took two steps forward and aimed the cannon in his direction. Sparks swirled in the barrel of what was obviously a Tesla cannon. That was not good.

Kaiden whipped out his barrier and managed to activate it a split-second before the cannon fired. He didn't have time to set it and instead, held it like a shield against the blast that surged toward him. Lightning pounded into it and he was hurled back as his protection disintegrated. He continued to somersault down the small hummock he had stood on and finally stopped when it leveled out.

His visor wiped the dirt away automatically as he sat and coughed from the force of the impact to prompt his breathing again. He picked Sire up as he stood and charged a shot.

The massive droid barreled down on him from the rise and he glanced hastily around for something that might offer refuge. The wide plain-like surroundings that had given them the advantage before only offered rocks and a couple of trees. In an instant, it had flipped to a severe disadvantage.

"Good God, this got intense fast."

"You should have simply enjoyed the knick-knacks," Chief chided. *"That looks like an old Dragoon model war machine. You might wanna leg it."*

"Do you have any bright ideas?" Kaiden asked as he looked back and fired. The plasma ball struck his target effectively but a barrier shimmered around it. "Shit. I guess the Halos still do have a few toys worth something."

"You still have a good chance to beat this thing, though. That barrier is built to withstand electric attacks and explosions, but Sire has more punch. More plasma shots should break through. Then we can worry about the weapons or maybe do the job with a couple of thermals."

"Gotcha. I'm on it." He glanced at his belt and counted three thermal grenades. "Shit. What if Genos is dealing with one too?"

"The comm interference could be coming from this thing or the guys in the junker," Chief pointed out. *"Get rid of it and see if you can contact him. Right now, you gotta be a soldier and not a leader. You'll only get killed if you don't pay attention."*

He nodded. The Dragoon was surprisingly fast and caught up easily as he raced from any cover he could find to the next and fired on it all the while. It retaliated with its turrets while the cannon cooled. He could tell the lasers weren't strong, but they fired so rapidly that his armor's shielding would be gone very quickly if he were caught, and it would be his organs not long after.

Kaiden looked ahead as he leapt down another ravine. He had very few options left and reasoned that he would have to get under it. Of course, he needed to be quick. Its barrier was weakening, but if the cannon was able to fire before he made it through, he would be lucky if he only caught the residual force. Even that could be a death sentence if he couldn't get up before the turrets fired again. He vented Sire once more.

"Chief, activate the battle suite."

The EI nodded in the HUD. The words **Battle Suite Engaged** flash across his display before his vision changed swiftly. He seemed to perceive everything clearer, time felt expanded, and all other the sense of time slowed. When his perception settled, he took a deep breath, slammed the vent closed, and backed away to aim his rifle upward. The earth shuddered as the Dragoon lumbered closer.

He lunged from his defensive position onto the side of the narrow ravine and across. On the other side, he spun and fired a shot at almost point-blank range when the droid tilted to look into the crevasse. It turned out to be a smart choice as its cannon had already begun to glow. The shot exploded and catapulted him away, but it destroyed the mechanical's barrier. It stumbled but righted itself quickly and rushed into the attack.

One of its legs raised to crush him, but he flung himself forward and into the shadow cast by the machine's leg above him and rolled under the huge body. He yanked one of his thermals free, activated it as hastily he could, and pitched it into the cannon. It vanished from sight and he immediately sprinted out of the way. The Dragoon tried to crush him with its back legs an instant before the thermal detonated. When the cannon erupted, the mechanical almost flipped on its back from the force. Kaiden smiled and turned to fire.

His plan, however, proved less effective than he'd hoped against his relentless adversary. The moment it regained its balance, it thundered in pursuit and swiped at him in wide arcs that either barely missed him or he was able to dodge by a hair's breadth. He retrieved another thermal but the turrets began to fire again and he was forced to weave and dance away from them. They weren't as precise as they had been previously and he was able to avoid them fairly easily, even given the short distance between him and the droid. He couldn't, unfortunately, earn himself a moment to stop and find an opening. Instead, he merely heaved it at his attacker and cursed when it was shot out of the air. Still, the machine recoiled from the explosion and the center separated to create a split in the middle that revealed a glowing blue orb.

"Get rid of it!" was Chief's only order.

Kaiden holstered Sire on his back and bolted up to the Dragoon, vaulted onto it, and whipped Debonair from his gauntlet. He pressed the barrel against the orb and held the trigger down until the gun began to burn and even cause sparks to fizzle from his shields. Eventually, it overheated and the mechanical monster began to thrash wildly. The motion jolted his pistol, which fell, but he held on and gritted his teeth. He located the melted frame around the light, grasped an edge, and yanked hard, taking Chief's advice literally. The orb was dragged out and he flung it aside. It was crushed by the machine's flailing limbs before it slowed and teetered ominously. The ace jumped off and it hobbled around and fired sporadically.

"That was definitely a power core. It must have multiple," Chief muttered.

"They must control some of the programs or what controls the machinery to keep it moving, walking around, and shaking," he observed. The battle suite had been on for more than four minutes and needed to end this soon.

He ran toward the Dragoon, retrieved Debonair, and slid the weapon into its compartment. His plasma blade activated on command and he slid beneath the stumbling war machine

"Hobble the bastard."

"That's the plan," he responded. The metal beast raised its leg and thrust it down violently. He almost felt like he was in slow motion and saw the angle of the strike and was able to guess how long before it reached him. At the perfect moment, he slid out of reach and kicked dust up but avoided the jagged metal. The claw on the massive foot landed behind him and sank into the dirt.

"Chief, what do I aim for?" he yelled.

"The yellow wires behind the top of the legs—onscreen!"

Kaiden hacked wildly at a few wires exposed by the fight and stabbed at connection points. He saw the wires highlighted by Chief in his display, hacked at the ones on the back legs, and sliced into the metal casing for good measure.

He grasped his last thermal, activated it, and left it behind when he rolled out and away. The Dragoon stumbled and collapsed, tried to balance itself on its two front legs for a moment, and finally crumpled in the dirt. One of the turrets turned to fire, but the explosion detonated beneath it. The body ruptured and caused a secondary explosion and the turret hung down, almost like the machine itself had admitted defeat.

The ace crawled back a few more yards before he stood and studied the mechanical. Its entire left side was destroyed and the remains of its legs strewn about the dusty field. Some of the lights were still active and the other turret shook and spun slowly to one side before it snapped in the other direction.

"Deactivate the battle suite, Chief."

"Five minutes, twenty seconds. Not bad."

His vision returned to normal, his read-outs appeared onscreen again, and Chief appeared in the corner. *"How do you feel?"*

He felt no trace of a headache and his limbs felt normal, perhaps even a little lighter. "I'm accustomed to it by now."

"You're making gains, partner."

The turret tried to aim at him once more before it also deactivated and the last flickering lights faded. He chuckled. "I'll give it some respect for being a tough son of a bitch."

"Kaiden, are you there?" Genos asked frantically. The comms had evidently cleared.

The ace smiled. "'Course I am. No friend this time?"

His teammate chuckled. "My apologies, friend. I was beset by a group of Havoc droids and these seemed to be closer to normal standards than the original group."

"Havoc droids?" he asked and glanced at the defeated Dragoon.

"It appears they did send reinforcements in after all—or perhaps had a trap prepared would be more accurate," Genos suggested. "It's dealt with on my end and I'm on my way toward the entrance. Did anything happen on yours?"

He grinned at the Dragoon before he turned to make his way toward the gate. "Nah, nothing happened."

CHAPTER THIRTEEN

Merrick studied the hologram that displayed the companies under their control, the progression of certain missions, and a message that brought him considerable pleasure.

The sleeper cell had officially made its way into the World Council. One of the most important pieces was in place.

He turned at a knock on his door and sat at his desk before he called out for the person to enter. His servant, Cole, walked in and approached with a glass of cognac. "Good evening, sir. I've heard the good news."

The AO leader smiled and closed the hologram before he accepted the glass. "Yes, it's good news indeed. I was actually worried about how long it was taking." He took a sip and placed the glass on his desk. "With them in place, we'll have the time we need. More importantly, we'll have the council in check before the game even starts."

"Not checkmate, sir?" Cole asked.

"No, not quite yet," he conceded and traced his finger

on the rim of his glass. "Fortunately, I think Dario will be able to help with that once he's completed his current errand."

Zachary Baylor was incredibly close to falling asleep. His small monitor had remained unchanged for almost four hours and he had sat on his ass for a total of eight. Once the main shipping crew left for the day, almost nothing happened on his side of the dock. He'd been able to trade positions with his pal Billy when he grew frustrated with all the paperwork and bureaucracy involved in heading the security at the Icarus Station's cargo hold and was able to file for a change to night watch for shipping. Little did he realize that he would still be in a frustrating position, although this time, due to boredom rather than statistics.

Damn near nothing happened there. He called in to check with the rest of the night crew and stared at the nearly always blank screens. While it was easy money, it was hardly exciting. The most action he saw was when the occasional vagrant wandered over in a drugged daze or a group of kids tried to hack the pass terminal to get in and steal something from the hold as a trophy to brag about to their friends. Both could be run off with a quick beam of the flashlight and some loud, gruff words. What a way to live life on the edge.

He glanced at a static white hue in the corner of the monitor. It told him it was 12:32 a.m. and that he was a couple of minutes late for check-in, but that was as much the fault of the knuckleheads he worked with as is own.

They should have taken the opportunity to call in and save him the trouble, which had been discussed at the meeting the previous night. He grunted and reminded himself that he had taken the gig knowing he would merely end up being the world's most official-looking babysitter.

Zac sighed and picked up his comms device. "Boys this is Bay. Check-in." He released the talk button, folded his arms, and slipped the device around his ear. A full minute of silence brought no response from any of the eight team members. He should have been confused or worried but he knew them—good men but jokers, they grew as bored as he did and as the 'old man,' he was the target for most of their pranks and oddball routines. At any other time, he might have humored them, but he was in a foul mood and this was plain lazy.

The security chief verified the positions of the others on his tablet before he stowed it in his back pocket, retrieved his jacket, and slipped it on as he left his office and entered the freezing temperature of the terminal hallway. His station was only a little over one hundred yards from the warehouse bay, so it was really a quick jog, but after he gave the others a half-hearted tongue lashing, he might stick around to shoot the breeze.

He entered the main building and closed the heavy metal door behind him. It was dark as the policy to save energy was to use a minimum amount of lights after 11 p.m. Zach turned his flashlight on and called to his men. There was no response. He took a large breath to bellow once again but his voice caught in his throat. A sound now issued from the darkness. Someone was singing, but it didn't sound like anyone in his crew.

"You made me what I am today. I hope you're satisfied." The low-pitched voice seemed almost like a mixture of sing-speaking and humming. "You dragged and dragged me down, until the soul within me died." The large chamber of the bay made it difficult for him to really locate the voice but it definitely grew louder.

"You've shattered each and every dream. Fooled me right from the start," it continued. He paused in confusion when he turned the corner. While he could have sworn he had found the source, he now merely stared at a dead-end. "And though you're not true, may God bless you…" Shoes clicked on the linoleum and approached from behind him. "That's the curse of an aching heart…"

The chief turned slowly and stared at a man in a button-down black shirt, red suit jacket, and shiny leather shoes—the singer, no doubt. He looked at the security officer with a lazy smile. A white-gloved hand removed a silver box from his lapel, took a small cigar out, and put it to his lips.

Zach grimaced, rested his free hand on his belt, and shined the flashlight on the intruder's face. "Am I supposed to applaud?" he asked wryly. The singer didn't even bother to shield his eyes and merely chuckled and gave a little bow.

"Did you like it? I'm certainly no professional but I like to think I can carry a tune." He looked out the window into the blackness of space. "When I see such beautiful sights like this, the mood simply feels right—it captivates me, you understand?" he continued, genuinely sincere. He took a drag from his cigar and Zach did a double-take. When had he lit it up? Smoke billowed from him as he released an overdramatic exhale. "My work now is a little different, but I used to love being around the entertainers and artists. Old habits and all that lead me to approach everything with a little flair."

He had already grown to despise this snarky asshole, and if this was the friend of one of the other security officers, he would have words with the culprit. "All right, Mr Showbiz, you need to go. This is a private sector and if you do not leave the premises immediately, I will call the station security on you." Sweat appeared on his brow for no apparent reason and he wondered how had it gotten warm so suddenly. He scratched his neck and pinpricks trickled in the wake of his fingers.

The stranger nodded and after another drag and plume of smoke, he retorted, "I'm actually here for a pickup, good sir. My shipment came in through 'unconventional' means and I have to come here personally."

The chief gave him a suspicious look. Had this man actually admitted to smuggling? He removed a small towel from a compartment on his belt and dabbed his face and neck. The unexpected heat had begun to bug him. He needed to check the heating system once he ran this jackass out. How had it gone from frigid to hot so rapidly?

"If you need to make a personal inquiry, come back in the morning and talk to someone. Until then, get the hell out of my...of my..." His tablet fell from apparently lifeless fingers and skittered across the floor. The heat had enveloped his entire body now. He fell, burning up, and no longer merely hot but as if he were truly ablaze. Flames seemed to surge through his veins and he wanted to scream but no sound escaped. He thrashed reflexively but his limbs would not respond. In horror, he realized that his legs were gone, turned to ash as the flames poured from him and crept up his body. Fire consumed his chest and licked at his face. He opened his mouth in a wordless scream before his vision darkened.

Dario walked up to what remained of Zach and took another drag as he picked up the man's tablet and confirmed that the others he had already dealt with were still displayed as alive. Good. The program he'd used to trick the system had worked, at least. He addressed the pile of ash while any remaining nanos returned to their compartments.

"I would have continued this conversation if you weren't so grumpy. Your coworkers, at least, humored me for a time." He turned and walked away before he stopped abruptly and looked over his shoulder. "Before you go, you wouldn't happen to know where the shipping manifests are kept, would you?" He grinned at the fading cinders of the corpse strewn along the floor. "So much for that."

The assassin approached a large metal container and snapped his fingers, and the lock fell off with satisfying pop. The door opened for him. He walked inside and saw his prize, a chrome box with ornate detailing across the top and the emblem of a blinded snake eating its tail in the style of the ouroboros stamped on top. Satisfied, he stepped outside and tapped a number on his phone. He hummed to himself while he waited for his contact to answer.

"Evening. It's Dario." He leaned against the container door. "I've received your package. Well done, Jensen, that's great detailing. But I really don't need to lug this thing around with me, do I? You only need the box inside the box... Hold on, I'll check." He snapped his fingers once more and the chest opened with a soft click. A small, featureless black carton lay inside.

"Yeah, it's there. I beg your pardon? Of course not. There won't be a trace. I'm a professional and I take great care in my work, *compagno*," he asserted. He stretched his gauntleted hand lazily. Amber lights sparked and spun away in all directions before they faded. In an instant, an inferno burst into existence around him. Dario casually retrieved the smaller box and strolled leisurely toward the exit.

"No, no trouble at all. I was a little bored and played with the staff first but they were not too entertaining. Nothing like the last mission Merrick sent me on." The fire raged and now swept through the rooms to devour everything in its path as he strolled with an almost dance-like grace to the door.

"No, I am not being ungrateful, but Merrick promised me a good mission after I did his little chore and he then made you do it for him? I swear he's become so obsessed with the mission. Almost as robotic as the Asitons," he grumbled as he stepped outside the bay that was now about to collapse in on itself. The alert already blared around the station "Hmm, the port? There may be some residual damage. It depends on how fast the boys in yellow do their thing. This is a relatively new station so things may not be quite at the ready." He opened a door that led into the dark tunnels of the maintenance halls and chuckled. "You should have come. The smell of a warm fire on a fall night is truly magical." A screen appeared in his HUD to display firefighters and security rushing to the bays. Orders barked and yells filled the air as they rushed to extinguish the blaze.

"But enough about me. Is there anything new going on in Australia? Oh, really now? Poland? What are you doing there?" He nodded after Jensen's response. "I see. Well, I'm obviously between gigs now. I could show up to offer 'incentive' if that helps. No? You don't like me that close, do you?"

At a large explosion, one of the camera feeds cut off. From the other, it seemed that the personnel raced toward the fire in their efforts to rescue personnel trapped by the unexpected blast. He chuckled and returned to his call. "Something ignited in the bay. Ten gets you twenty it was a smuggled shipment of chems. That should make the evening more festive." As he continued down the path, the sounds of the fire faded at his back and the darkness of the tunnels consumed his path ahead.

"I guess I'll have to make my own fun for a while. Tell me, Jensen, were you playing a part when Kaiden's EI was a hot topic? Not so much? I have to say he's become such a strong fighter since the initial vids. I may have been a little cocky, but it's been so long since I've had a good fight. I can't wait for round two myself."

While the other man spoke, Dario thought back to Kaiden and wondered if he should make the effort to target him. Technically, Merrick still wanted the EI. As if his boss had read his mind, he was notified that he had received a message from the man. Amused, he opened and read it. "I'm sorry Jensen. I'll have to let you go. It seems the *capo* has a real mission for me now. Doing what?" He smiled and sauntered on through the darkness. "He's letting me do what I do so well, of course."

With that, he ended the call and began to sing once more—merrily, too as he recalled the screams that had long since faded.

CHAPTER FOURTEEN

Magellan lit a cigarette in the shadow of the outpost's eaves. He wasn't worried about the low light of his habit giving his position away to any guards in the complex in the distance, not in this dark, howling downpour. He might have been concerned about the smell alerting the guards in the outpost itself but considering that two out of the three were tranquilized in the one-man-sized bathroom and the third was locked inside the supply closet, knocked unconscious after a short chat, they weren't an issue.

"He really should have made the recording first time around." he murmured before he took another drag. "You find two of your buddies on the floor and you think the guy responsible is willing to negotiate?" He smirked and uttered a slow, gravelly chuckle. "If you're going to pretend you have guts, at least don't scream that loudly when someone grabs you by the shoulder." He exhaled and a grey plume of smoke drifted slowly on the frigid night air. It disintegrated into a haze to frame the Normandy Co building before him. He had observed the company's head-quarters over the last four days, blending in with groups of investors, potential clients, and even tourists who came to see the structure that was the oldest established company among the stars—as far as they knew anyway.

To pass the time, he wondered if every individual working there was corrupt or if it was merely a handful puppeteering a poor group of innocents. He believed it was the latter, as it was far too easy to get numerous photos and blueprints from them by simply masquerading as a tourist and being able to find easy access and getaway points. His tablet rumbled and he retrieved it to read another message from his dealer. The CEO—the 'lovingly' eccentric Oliver Solos—who had hired him wanted another update. It had only been an hour since his last one.

The bounty hunter leaned back and considered the meeting. Solos came off as...wrong, for lack of a better term. He'd said this was a retrieval mission, that he had a stake in the company and was currently at odds with the other stockholders but needed something taken back.

Both experience and instinct joined ranks to make him utterly certain he was being played.

"So you see, Mister..." Count Oliver Solos trailed off as he poured another generous serving of wine into a freakishly large glass. The man honestly might as well simply use the bottle.

"Magellan. And if you forget again, feel free to look at

my liquor cabinet you took that one-thousand-credit wine from," he suggested. While he tried to sound somewhat jovial, he masked his sarcasm poorly. He set his feet on his desk and motioned to a chair in front of him. "Do you care to sit down, sir? I need to hear all the details you can provide before I agree."

The man raised an eyebrow, his expression scornful. "You act as if I have held something back. If you can't understand my proposal, I don't see how that is any error of mine." He sat, however, and slid a hand inside the pocket of his jacket to retrieve a small box decorated in red and yellow, adorned with symbols that looked like a serpent eating its own tail.

"My apologies." The bounty hunter sighed. "But I can only gather so much from what you've told me. In fact, I have to say I can't see a reason why you need me specifically. If this device is yours and you have a stake in Normandy, go and reclaim it."

Oliver snorted with contempt. "You don't get much work, do you?" He took a cigar from his ornate box, lit it, and smoke drifted in a slow, lazy cloud. "At least not with a pompous attitude like that."

Magellan eased his hand toward the lower drawer of his desk and silently unlocked the tab to snake his fingers to the gun therein. "I don't have too many billionaires coming through my doors—at least, not in person. I'm willing to hear you out, but I'm a high-ranked bounty hunter. I can't afford to take a gig that could end up with me as a wanted man."

"I can assure you that I am asking no such thing!" The man hissed outrage. "And I can also assure you that it angers me that you would make such an accusation."

He gripped the handle of his pistol and the metal of its hilt against his palm cooled the heat of his anger, at least a little. "My apologies," he said and clenched his teeth. "It is obvious that this means much to you, so I am willing to hear you out. If you can begin again, please?"

"Fine, fine. Very well, I shall repeat myself, if only because my request is so important to me and my legacy." Oliver took another drag followed by a sip, his expression one of long-suffering. "Give me a moment. Every time I think about this travesty, I think I might lose my mind and die."

"I've learned I'm never that lucky." Magellan huffed under his breath and willed his hand to move from his gun to his own cigarette case. "I'll give you all the time you need. I mean that. Please, take at least until the sun sets."

"That's not for another two hours."

"I'm aware." He lit his cigarette and relaxed into his chair before he took a moment to study the aristocrat in front of him. Oliver might be insufferable as a person but he played the high-society role well. He was aided in this by long blond hair, light to the point of being white, a tall brow, sunken cheeks, and plucked, narrow eyebrows atop deep-green eyes. The eyes had rather obviously had work done on them. They had a low-light glow and the shade of color would slowly lighten to a pleasant green that reminded him of the plains of the planet Panrama. In the next moment, they would darken to a shadowy jungle-green. The bounty hunter's best guess was that he used these for seduction and he wondered if he should ask if they worked at all. It might be handy in his own job.

His potential client was dressed in a buttoned, long jacket decorated like his cigar box—red body with golden trim and buttons. His slacks and heeled boots were both a solid black. He couldn't make out the material in the dim light but considering the near-perfect fit and personal attention to the stitching, they must have cost more than some of the guns Magellan owned.

"Well, I'm sorry to disappoint you, but I seem to have miraculously composed myself."

"Wonderful," he muttered and took a quick drag. "So, what is the story?" The businessman sipped from his glass and moved his hair from his face so he could stare demurely at the bounty hunter.

"What I am after is not a device," he began and straightened his posture. "It would seem that some of my...associates have skulked about my various companies. In particular, my main building outside of town. Some of my personal guard and my more astute personnel have begun to notice new hires who were somehow brought on board without the knowledge of myself or any of my management. Furthermore, some of my handlers in more...shall we say private divisions have noticed an increase in visitors to the city that can be traced back to more nefarious yet profitable professions."

Magellan allowed himself a smirk. "You mean people like me?"

"I did not wish to come right out and say it, but I assumed you would grasp my meaning." He gave a wry smile before he swallowed the last of his drink. "Normally,

I would simply allow my peons to erase the correct documents and my network to go out and deal with the interlopers as they saw fit—you know, typical business. However, we have discovered that these shady individuals may, in fact, be after material that is not so easily recoverable." He reached out once again to grab the bottle of wine, but his host shot him a glare. A scowl formed on Oliver's face but he withdrew his hand.

"So, some of your competitors are looking to steal from you and may have potentially hired less than upstanding lackeys to do the deed. Even if we factor in that some of your associates may have been involved, I don't see how this leads you—a wealthy and…upstanding man—to decide that it's a good idea to come to me personally. After all, you must have more than enough resources to deal with the scum without having to resort to my measures?" He took the bottle and a small glass from his desk. Once he'd poured a little, he left about a quarter and passed it to the other man. He took it—albeit with a cautious hand—and emptied what remained into his glass.

"Mr. Magellan, I'm beginning to think you believe I lack foresight or, at the very least, think me an idiot."

He simply narrowed his eyes until the CEO took the hint. "I am a gentleman. I will not lie, so yes." He finished his drink in one swallow. "Although I'm cynical enough to realize that running an empire must take more than charisma and expensive taste alone. So now that I know the story, tell me… What's my part?"

Something occurred, then, that briefly knocked him out of his scornful attitude. Oliver's demeanor changed, although it would not have been obvious to most. A small smile formed on his lips and his body language revealed virtually nothing, but the haughty air of the snob seemed to vanish. His pose turned cold, and his shifting eyes seem to, on instinct, change to their darker shade.

"Because there are only two ways for me to get what I want. Either I can have someone fetch the information and items I need and return them to me. Or I need the problem erased." His nonchalant tone disappeared to be replaced by a frosty edge. He spoke in a way that made every word sound like liquid pouring from his mouth. "I need someone who cannot be traced back to me, someone who already has a reputation for dealing with the shady areas of life and for doing deeds most dirty for anyone with the right credits."

He finished his drink and set the empty glass down before he placed his elbows on the desk, intertwined his fingers, and rested his chin upon them. "You are right that I heard of you through gossip. But you also know gossip has a nasty habit of fabrication and mucking up the truth. I need someone who can get in and retrieve something quite valuable to me at great risk to themselves, and from what I heard, you would be an excellent choice. If those rumors were untrue, the fault is on me—although it would be such a pity to think that a man like you could not back them up."

The light from the office's window dimmed as the sun sank slowly from the sky and cast a dusky light on the two men. Magellan began to feel uneasy. Something told him this man was a danger. From his appearance, he shouldn't be able to generate such a feeling of dread. He didn't like this—neither the job nor the man.

"Do you use it well?" the CEO asked with a smirk and gestured at one of the rifles on the wall.

The bounty hunter glanced at the weapon while he eased his other hand to the pistol. "I can give you a demonstration if you like."

"I'd rather you put it into action," He chuckled, leaned forward, and rested his chin on the back of his hands. "If you accept this, I shall leave you with a location where you can place my little trinket that I will be sure to reward you most handsomely for—three million credits upon completion and another two million should you return undetected." Oliver leaned back into his chair while Magellan considered that figure. "If you fail, I can use you as an excuse to have my guard professionally move my belongings under the disguise of a break-in and place the blame on you—or, rather, your corpse." The grin widened, giving the man's once well-composed face the look of madness. "I shall even promise you a beautiful funeral."

"What a kind gesture—" His eyes narrowed in confrontation. He knew he should back out, but even if the man only spoke partial truths, he wanted to know what was happening behind the scenes. When shady businesses dealt in the dark, it could cause problems for more than only them. If nothing else, he might find a reason to pursue the bastard himself. "Consider this my acceptance, Mr. Solos."

Oliver smiled and raised his hands. He clapped three times and a gray-haired, white-suited servant—or perhaps a bodyguard, given his size—entered the office. He walked to Oliver's side and produced a small book—a journal it seemed—and handed it to the bounty hunter, who began to flip through the archaic ledger.

"Feel free to read that whenever you please. It contains a few notes, pictures, and the like. I prefer to keep all the necessary and important information on paper. It's less likely to be stolen. As I insinuated, I don't have an issue with you taking whatever action necessary, but if you could do me a favor..." He looked up from the book and raised an eyebrow. "Do try to reduce the bloodshed, at least in the building. It is such a beautiful, storied place and blood is tricky to clean. I would hate to have it sullied."

"You mean more than you already have?" The words left his mouth before he could filter them. The assistant stiffened and the man's jaw clenched in anger.

"I do not corrupt, I cultivate." The count stood, and a servant placed a crimson jacket on him that he had folded across his arm. "My best wishes to you, Magellan. The location for the meeting is in the back of the book. I look forward to your return, in person." He moved to leave the office but paused at the doorway and leaned a hand on the frame. "Unfortunately, my final word is a warning. Should that devious little head of yours contemplate the idea of making off with my files, I can promise you that I will not extend any patience to you. I will retrieve what is mine and enjoy the hunt as well." With that and a final dark look from the guard, they left. The bounty hunter sat in silence until the creeping moonlight illuminated his office.

Magellan was snapped out of his memories by another

message. This one, much more happily, was from Sasha. He opened and read it, and his eyes widened. Kaiden was going after an army? That had to be an exaggeration. He looked at the Normandy building in the distance, then back to the message. He remembered his promise and he would make good. Oliver could wait for now, and the idea of making him throw a fit was rather amusing, actually.

CHAPTER FIFTEEN

Genos and Kaiden made their way cautiously to the main gate. The large cannons above the doors had apparently come online while they were dealing with their previous attackers. The weapons glowed with a blue light visible from the opening and an audible electrical crackle indicated that they were probably modified Tesla cannons. Kaiden took a couple of steps back and realized they would probably have to find another entrance. He doubted that either he or Genos could hack the door while worrying about getting fried in a single shot.

The mechanist, however, continued to advance while he removed a grenade from his belt. He pressed the activation switch, holstered his cannon on his back, and drew a launcher. The cannons continued to charge as he slid the grenade into the launcher and fired calmly. When the device detonated, it burst apart and some kind of grey smoke appeared in one instant and vanished in the next. The Tsuna smiled and took a few steps forward.

The large weapons, now close to their peak, suddenly

shifted and spun to face the city they were meant to protect.

"Nano grenades?" the ace asked, bemused.

"Of course." His teammate nodded, stowed the launcher, and folded his hands behind his back. "They are quite useful. Those cannons aren't particularly advanced and seem to be created from scavenged parts like most of the other contraptions we've come across. That makes them very easy to manipulate with nanos."

Kaiden flipped his rifle and rested it on his shoulder. "Out of curiosity, what if they were too advanced for the nanos to control? Did you have another plan?"

The mechanist nodded. "I'm sure it was the same as yours—running."

He chuckled. "Should we fire a few warning shots?"

"That doesn't seem very diplomatic." Genos shrugged. "I'll have Viola keep them ready, but unless our hosts try something, I'll simply keep them in position."

"Attention hostiles!" a voice cried from a speaker system along the walls.

"I think they're trying something." Kaiden grinned while his teammate folded his arms patiently.

"We respect how far you've come, but know that we will not let you in. You have forced us to use our last line of defense. We are currently preparing our satellite cannon to fire upon you. The explosion radiates for up to five miles."

"I assume this is a bluff?" Genos asked and glanced at his friend.

"Oh, yeah, a big one," he confirmed. "No one is allowed to have sat-cannons anymore. That's been a rule ever since the WC was officially recognized. I doubt they could actually make one and even if they did, the military would have scorched this place long before we got here."

"If you do not turn back now, we will fire the cannon and vaporize you where you—"

"Excuse me!" Genos shouted and waved.

"Uh, what?" the voice demanded.

"If you did fire this cannon and the radius of the explosion was as vast as you said, wouldn't you also catch your own base in the blast?" he reasoned.

"Um, may— No? No! We'll fire the blast behind you so you'll be caught in the wave with no chance to escape."

"Uh-huh." Kaiden rolled his eyes. He motioned for Genos to follow as they both made their way closer to the gate.

"What are you doing?" the voice asked.

"Look, either fire the cannon or open the gate," he demanded when they stood directly in front of the door and leaned against it. "We're not here to pillage or kill anyone if that's the concern. We want to talk."

"Really? You could have been a little more civil then."

"You fired on us," the Tsuna pointed out.

"You didn't send any messages that you were approaching!"

"Because you fired on us," Kaiden retorted and shook his head. "Let me extend a branch here. I don't think I know their names but check if anyone remembers an incident with a droid that annihilated a good chunk of your forces and was destroyed by a merc."

"Wait, huh? What are you... Hold on... Fritz? Stole Kit's jet-bike?"

"Oh, good, they do remember me."

"Is that a good or bad thing?" his friend asked.

"*A little of both, really,*" Chief interjected and appeared in both their HUDs. "*They might open the gate simply for a chance to kill him.*"

"That still seems mostly bad," Genos reasoned.

"Okay, the leaders remember you all right." The voice grunted in what might have been disapproval. "You don't have to worry about the cannon. But they are quite curious about why you're back, and they seem— Oh, too much?"

"Good Lord, who's on this shift?" Kaiden muttered.

"Opening the gate!"

He pushed off the door as it began to rumble and it sank below ground to reveal the junk town within, along with another group of droids. His brow furrowed as he prepared Sire and Genos drew his cannon. Fortunately, the mechanicals began to retreat, then turned to either side of the street with their heads down. The mechanist glanced quickly at him and he shrugged in response but didn't holster his weapon. He took a few tentative steps and the droids didn't react, but at the end of the street, a manhole cover was pushed aside and a man in his early twenties with a blue ponytail and armor crawled out. He stood, brushed himself off, and waved for them to approach. "Hey there. Name's Falco."

"Howdy." Kaiden recognized the voice. "You were the one on the speakers?"

"Yeah. I'm not supposed to be but you guys appeared between shifts and I happened to be in the room while everyone else was scrambling."

"Well, I promise that you were really convincing." He chuckled. "Are your bosses ready to see me?"

"Yeah, I'm to lead you to them." Falco scratched the back of his head. "Listen, there's a couple of things I wanted to say before you meet, though."

"Such as?" Genos inquired.

"Well, they do remember you. I was only brought in about six months ago—long after all that stuff with the killer droid happened—so I'm not really up to speed. But I should mention that they seem to be...uh, rather pissed with you."

The ace frowned. "I didn't exactly think things would be rosy, but I did spare them and save their HQ from their own fuck up, didn't I?"

"You also electrocuted them, I think?" Falco reminded him carefully.

He thought back and nodded quickly. "That too."

"They seem mostly angry about that—along with stealing Kit's bike and not leaving anything salvageable from the droid."

"I dropped a building on it," he retorted. "The only thing left was the head, and I had to take it in to show that I actually destroyed it."

"Do you recall what company made that droid?" Genos asked.

"Not off the top of my head," he replied with a quick look at his teammate. "Why?"

"I'm curious. It's something to look into later."

"Either way, I wanted to make sure you guys really aren't here to simply ransack the place," Falco explained.

Kaiden almost burst out laughing. "I've seen and tried many different tactics. Polite requests is still a new one for me."

"We have no ill intentions," the Tsuna promised.

"If you need proof, well…" The ace shrugged and gestured at the weapons that still aimed at the deserted city. "It seems all you guys have left is a few droids, and we have access to the cannons. If we wanted to cause trouble, we could do that rather easily."

"It's kind of an asshole way to put it, but you are right," the man admitted. "Look, most of us here are new recruits. The Azure Halos have been rebuilding, but the newer members are more into engineering and mechanics than hacking."

He frowned. "Damn, we're actually here looking for hackers."

"We still have a couple of dozen, maybe a little more, and some of the guys are multi-talented, but all the same —" He scratched the back of his head again sheepishly. "What I'm trying to say is that if you're here because of some hacking trouble or an old grudge, we'd really like to not be caught in the crossfire."

Kaiden shook his head. "Again, that's not the issue here. If anyone shoots first, it'll be your bosses."

"You could try your best to make sure that doesn't happen," Genos suggested. "You know how your…discussions can get."

"I'll try my best to keep it civil," he promised. "We need their help, after all."

"I guess that's the best I can hope for." Falco shrugged and gestured vaguely toward the gate. "One more thing before we go. About the cannons…"

"Hmm? Oh, yes." The mechanist nodded and looked back for a moment. The cannons spun so they no longer faced toward the city and powered down. "For safety, I'll continue to control them as long as we're here unless the meeting takes longer than my nanos can sustain."

"About how long is that?" Kaiden asked.

"For these models, about another seventy minutes."

He nodded and then followed as their young guide slid back into the sewers. "Hopefully it shouldn't, but if things get heated...Chief, you should probably bring the ship closer."

"Oh, I did that as soon as you walked into the gate," the EI informed him. *"I also know how your discussions can go."*

"Like I said, I'll be civil." As soon as he had descended the ladder, another group of havoc droids stood and stared at him. They didn't prepare to fire but seemed ready to if he tried anything. He sighed and shook his head. "They aren't making it easy, though."

CHAPTER SIXTEEN

When they finally entered what they assumed to be the closest thing the Halos had to a central command, they were greeted by a room that was vastly different than the shantytown above. Holoscreens abounded. A number of members either worked on tech or repaired armor and droids. Wires and glowstrips littered surfaces and various monitors displayed schematics, messages, or diagnostic check completion rates. This looked more like the place a hacker or tech gang would work in.

"It looks pretty good, right?" Falco asked as they continued to pass through.

"Yeah. If you guys actually still have funds for stuff like this, you'd think you'd use a little of it above," Kaiden stated and made no effort to hide the slight challenge in his tone.

Falco turned and began to walk backward as he continued. "The Junk Town is basically a front. Even before the incident, that's how it was," he explained. "Of course, some of the buildings are powered up and function as labs or repair shops to keep up appearances or when we need the space. But most are filled with proxy servers and the like to confuse any other gangs or even military who decide to prod around over the net."

He nodded. "That's neat, but should you really tell us that?"

The young man stopped in his tracks, thought it over for a moment, and finally lowered his head and sighed. "Dammit."

"You're not paid very well, are you?" The ace chuckled.

"Falco!" a voice shouted. The trio looked up the hall to see a man with slicked-back blue hair and angry eyes. Kaiden recognized him, albeit vaguely. "You were one of those I talked to after beating the droid."

The man approached and studied him carefully. "Yeah, my name's Fritz." He scowled. "I should pound you for doing us a dirty like that."

"Feel free to try," he said lightly and tapped the stock of his rifle. "But you know that droid did you dirtier."

Fritz scowled but shrugged and nodded. "That's why we're talking at all. Follow me, Falco, you're dismissed."

The kid nodded. "Right, sir." He turned and whispered as he passed. "Please remember to not start anything, all right?"

"Yeah, yeah," he muttered as he and Genos followed the other man into a makeshift conference room. A woman with long black hair with several blue dyed lines glowered at him and her bright eyes revealed EI lenses. The other occupant was a tall, thin man with close-cropped hair—

streaked black and white—who wore a long blue jacket with the Halos logo on the chest.

"Hello again," he stated as Fritz took a seat belligerently beside him. "You've met Fritz now. I am Janis, and this is Kit." He pointed to the woman, who nodded coolly.

"I guess we didn't really have a chance for introductions last time," Kaiden admitted as he and his companion sat and removed their helmets. "I'm Kaiden Jericho, ace in training at Nexus academy, and this is Genos, a Tsuna mechanist."

"Nexus Academy as well?" Janis asked and looked at the Tsuna.

"Indeed." Genos nodded.

"So we were showed up by an Academy kid?" Fritz sighed. "That'll look great for our rep."

"I'm twenty-two," he replied. "And I was here for the droid, not for you."

"If the droid was not active, you probably would have dealt with us instead, right?" Janis asked.

"Technically, I suppose. But I remember you saying that most of you didn't want the droid turned on. I could probably have talked you into giving it to me instead of…more violent methods."

"I doubt that was the first plan you came up with," the Halo leader countered and leaned forward. "But you seem to be saying that more to placate us than anything else. You said you wanted to talk. What about?"

"First off, that jet-bike—who's was that again?"

"It was mine," Kit said and finally spoke. "Do you know where it is, by any chance?"

"Uh, probably in pieces in a chop shop. I sold it for

creds a couple of towns away after I left," he confessed and she narrowed her eyes. He raised his hands defensively. "I wanted to start this by offering to pay for it. It seems only fair to try to wash away at least a little of the bad blood."

She considered this, folded her arms, and after a long moment, slid into a chair. "We can talk about that after we talk about whatever you're here for."

"Right, so…" He clapped to focus his thoughts and find the best words. Unlike the Riders and Kings, he wasn't exactly on good terms with the Halos, which made the offer difficult now that he actually had to voice it. "I need hackers—although, from what I understand, you've…uh, branched out?"

"After a fashion," Janis responded vaguely.

"Not by choice, really." Fritz huffed. "After the massacre, only a little over a dozen of us were left to pick up the pieces. We had enough funds to scrape together new hires, but the other divisions of the Halos in the west were wary about joining up with us, even temporarily to help. The guys we were able to get were either new to the whole gang life deal or were from smaller gangs looking to make their way up." He chuckled and shook his head. "Some bounced when they got here and saw the state of everything "

"That room outside is mostly made up of what we salvaged from before the droid attacked. Most of it is actually older stock we kept in inventory," Kit informed them. "We're making some headway, but if you need hackers…I guess it depends on the job."

Kaiden was rather surprised. He definitely hadn't expected to get an earful of their current predicament but assumed they hadn't really had the chance to actually voice how screwed they were after the attack. They obviously had to keep up appearances for the newbies. A gang having to hope that their previous reputation was enough to sustain them was common after a bad loss.

"Then I guess I'll get to the point," he began. "I'm building an army—a group of raiders, really." He extended his hand and Chief appeared. Fritz and Janus went wide-eyed and Kit looked at it curiously. She was the only one with EI lenses and he sometimes forgot that being able to see an EI without some kind of device was odd. Chief turned into a hologram of the AO fortress—the old one Kaiden knew. "It's run by a group that's looking to cause considerable trouble for everyone," he explained. "They've been making moves, mostly capturing big businesses through both legal means and very much illegal. After that, it looks like they plan to move into terrorist actions."

"What kind?" the Halo leader demanded. "I know 'terrorist' is never good, but it can come in many varieties."

"We don't exactly know yet. But it is one that they are building quite a big army for, and it seems my school might be one of the first targets." The hologram changed to display different models of droids. "We don't know everything they are building, but we do know they seem to be amassing a hell of a force. This fortress seems to be one of their main barracks and development stations."

"That looked...big," Fritz muttered. "You wanna take that place on?"

"We don't have the forces to take on something like that," Kit pointed out. "Even at our prime, we're not an—"

"Assault force. I know. That's not the plan for you," he

countered. "Like I said, I need hackers. I'm sure they have human defenders of some kind, but the majority of what we face will be droids and automated defenses. I have a couple of hackers already, but with how big this place is and how this could go to hell really quickly, having backup and a larger team of hackers would be helpful. You wouldn't have to be with the main force at all. I have the Fire Riders and Skyway Kings for that, along with some other friends."

"The Riders and Kings?" Janis whispered, his face creased in thought. "You have yourself quite the force already. You really seem to want to do this."

"I'll ask the big question if you don't mind, Janis," Fritz stated and fixed his stare on Kaiden. "If this place is such a danger, why not contact the military? Why are you planning this with a group of gang members?"

"Because this organization is good at hiding themselves and have done so for years." He remained silent for a moment and tried to decide if it was better to reveal what he knew or if that would simply make them laugh it off. They'd believed him this far, though. "Have you heard of the Arbiter Organization?"

"The new Illuminati, essentially?" Fritz asked. He glanced at his Halo teammates and they both nodded. "Yeah, we have."

"Are you saying this is their base?" Janis questioned and focused on the hologram as the droid figures shrunk and the base was displayed behind them. "That's…rather foreboding if true."

"I'm not sure how many they have." The ace sighed. "My team and I took care of a smaller one but from what we know, they have a few more like that. But this is the biggest one we've found and the most important one we're aware of. We want to not only eliminate it from the field, but we hope we can find something concrete there—plans, a ledger, or relevant data. We need something we can show the council that will make them take action before the AO does."

"I see." Janis leaned back in his chair. "Before we go further, what are you offering?"

"As in pay?" he asked and received a nod in response. "Whatever you can carry with you. All I want—what my team wants—is the evidence."

"Did you make the same promise to the other gangs?" Kit asked.

"I did," he confirmed. "But as hackers, you'll be in the building first and have more time to gather what you wish when the fighting finishes. Plus, you're probably the only ones who will want what's on the servers. The others can't hack into them like you can."

"They can simply take the computers, though, which are still worth creds as equipment," Fritz argued. "Although, I suppose a couple of us could probably strip them before they think of that themselves."

Fritz, Janis, and Kit looked at one another, almost like they had a silent conversation. Their leader finally drew a deep breath and turned to Kaiden. "We have ten high-class hackers and about twenty more that can help with more moderate objectives—splicing into doors, commandeering defense, and the like. Our Engineers can help with the assault, along with the droids."

"How many droids?" Genos asked.

"And of what caliber?" The ace looked out of one of the windows of the room to where a few assault droids were being assembled with junk parts. "It looks like most will be fodder."

"Most of the droid force will be," the man agreed. "But we have a shipment of parts and mods coming from the other Halo division in Oregon. We'll be able to assemble a small force of Havoc, Guardian, and Soldier droids that will actually be able to mount a solid offense."

"When will the attack happen?" Fritz asked.

"We're still putting the final pieces together." He retrieved his tablet. "Do you have a contact?"

Janis nodded and picked up his own tablet and they exchanged information. "I'll keep you informed, but estimate another week of preparation at a minimum."

"That should be enough to assemble a stronger force."

"I'll make sure everyone works day and night to get it together," Kit promised.

"Make sure not to work them too hard," Fritz warned. "They need to be ready to fight and hack too."

"Then we're agreed?" Kaiden asked and a little of the weight left his chest.

Janis nodded. "Obviously, we're not exactly altruistic, but I assume that even if this isn't some organization of rumors, they are still assembling a force that is worrying. If they are attacking your Academy, my guess that's only a start before they tear across the country, which includes us."

"I'm sure the military would get involved, even if they found some way to hold them off," Kit reasoned. "But who knows how much land they can cover in that time?"

"Plus all the goods we can get from this," Fritz added with a smirk. "It'll be nice to work with new tech again."

Kaiden and Genos nodded and the ace shook Janis' hand. "Thanks for listening, and…uh, sorry for shocking you back then."

"A little static between temporary allies." The man chuckled and his grasp tightened a little. "No worries."

He nodded and looked at Kit. "So, what do I owe you?"

"I'll send you the bill later," she stated. "I have other concerns than jet bike shopping for now."

"Understood. We'll be off, then." Kaiden and Genos went to the door and the ace paused as he pulled it open. "Oh, right. Are you guys gonna bring that sat-cannon too?"

He looked back to see Fritz's amused face, but the humor wasn't shared by Janis and Kit.

"I'll take that as a no. I'm looking forward to the battle!" he called as they hurried out of the underground base.

CHAPTER SEVENTEEN

Genos took manual control of the ship from Chief and prepared to take off. Kaiden exhaled a relieved sigh as he took his co-pilot chair.

"That wasn't so bad, was it?" The Tsuna chuckled as the ship began to gain altitude.

"Maybe not for us, but if we were simply some nice elders there to tell them the good news, we'd be paste by now," he joked.

"I'm not really sure what that means," his companion replied as the ship banked away from the Halos base. "But I'll agree with you, nonetheless." Genos increased speed with a suddenness that made Kaiden flatten himself against his seat. The junk town seemed to rocket into the distance.

As he virtually pried himself off the chair and forced his muscles to relax, he noticed a blinking light in the corner of his vision. "What's that, Chief?"

"Messages. You have quite a few."

The blinking stopped but a panel of contacts appeared in its place. Two were from Zena and Janis, checking the number to make sure it was right, but the seventeen others weren't.

"What the hell? Laurie and Chiyo have been trying to reach me," he exclaimed.

"Oh…I suppose we should have checked in with them through all this, shouldn't we?" his teammate murmured.

"Chief, why didn't any of these get through?"

"They did but I held them off."

"Why?" he demanded.

Chief's eye narrowed in exasperation. *"We have been kind of dealing with more important things the last few hours—you know, like getting shot. I sent them messages saying call back later but they didn't listen."*

"They're probably wondering how the meetings went." He sighed and tried to contact Chiyo. "At least we'll have good news to send back."

The comm link took a moment to establish but she answered quickly and he opened a holoscreen. "Nice of you to finally return," she began, a snarky edge to her tone. "Where are you and what happened?"

"Good evening, friend Chiyo," Genos said cheerfully.

"Hello, Genos," she responded. "Answer the question, Kaiden."

He chuckled. She seemed peeved, for some reason. "I've had a little trouble, but it's all good now," he informed her.

"Trouble? Did the gangs attack you?" she demanded and worry replaced the grumbling.

"Not really. I would ask you to contact a cleaner if that were the case, and not the kind that makes your armor look fresh." He laughed. "The Fire Riders and Skyway

should have some good models by the time we are ready to go, but most are slightly better than junkers."

"Still, it's better than using humans as fodder," she reminded him. "That's actually a more sizeable force than I expected. Are they aware of what we're facing?"

"I told them the gist. They know this won't be easy but they've decided they can't let these guys run around freely. It's bad for business. That and the potential loot."

"Well, either for gain or morals, I'm glad we actually have their help," she confessed. "It makes it seem more possible now."

"What have you and Cyra found out?" he asked.

"We've been in training, mostly, but the professor told us something troubling."

"What's that?"

"The AO seems to be using Asiton tech," she revealed.

"Asiton?" Genos asked sharply and glanced quickly at the screen before he returned his focus to the window. "Those were the machines that caused a war, correct?"

"Yeah, about a hundred years ago now." Kaiden nodded. "Are they building new models or only retro-fitting scrap?"

"I'm not entirely sure. But they do seem to have some functioning models from the past."

The ace was sure those had been upgraded, but even for tech that was a nearly a century old, the Asitons were nothing to dismiss lightly. After all, he would know considering he'd fought with them a few times in the—Shit, were they testing them against him? He felt both anger and concern flare up in him but this was something he had to consider. If they were, he had survived and now had some experience fighting them. That could come in handy if they did have Asitons in their ranks.

"We'll have to make sure we let everyone know. But I'm sure their main force is still only droids, right?"

"Only droids? You are aware that all these droids are well armed and probably modified to well past what we're used to fighting?" Chiyo sounded a little acerbic.

Kaiden nodded and leaned back. "I'm sure you're right, but Julio said he would help us with arms and armor as well. I doubt even he can outfit everyone, but all the gangs have their own gear and I know the Kings and Riders won't skimp on that."

"Perhaps, but I know that you didn't plan for this to be a siege." she pointed out.

"True enough. Technically, you and the other hackers will be the main force." He ran a hand through his hair and closed his eyes. "I hate to put you in such a dangerous position. But if you can get in there and shut everything down —or even better, turn them against each other— that will win the day more than anything."

"Don't be sorry," she said. "That's what we're here to do."

The ace smiled. "You sound more like a soldier than a techie."

"Even logistics are trained for combat at Nexus," she replied with a smile of her own. "Our engineers especially —isn't that right, Genos?"

"Technically, my class is more battle-oriented than others so…" He looked over to see both his friends staring at him. "Ah, you meant that as a compliment. I agree."

Kaiden shrugged and his smile returned. "Hey, he has

idioms down for the most part. You can't knock him too hard."

"Yes, please don't," the Tsuna concurred.

"Cute, Genos."

"We can discuss more when we're all together," Chiyo said. "You both will be back in time for the feast, correct?"

"Oh, yeah. The finals feast," Kaiden recalled. "We wouldn't miss that. It's two nights away, right?"

"Yes. They are holding it early this year since many masters already have their operations ready and they can have an early start," she explained.

"I hope we can join them, but we still have things to put into place." He frowned and thought through the growing list. "Flynn and Cameron will give me hell for being late to the party."

"When we reveal that we were the ones to oust the organization, you can feel free to give them hell right back," she retorted. "Until then, I believe we should play it as safe as we can before that is no longer an option."

"Well said," he agreed. "See you soon—actually before you go, have you seen Sasha or Wolfson around?"

"Laurie mentioned meeting with them sometime soon. I assume to have a discussion much like ours."

He nodded. "We all need to meet at least a couple of times to go over everything, including the gang leaders. Although all the teachers said they were looking into things themselves. I wonder what they are talking about?"

CHAPTER EIGHTEEN

As soon as the commander walked into the private room, he was greeted by the professor's sing-songy tone. "Greetings, Sasha!"

Laurie and Wolfson sat across from each other in large chairs and he was almost irate that both seemed to take this rather lightly until he noticed neither of them had a glass or bottle in hand. Most people probably wouldn't have noticed but for Laurie, it was almost unheard of.

"Were you able to get in touch with that bounty hunter friend of yours?" Wolfson asked and gestured to the chair between the two for him to sit.

He nodded as he took his place. "He sent a message that he would be coming, but he's out at the moment."

"Out as in..." The large man raised an eyebrow in query.

"He didn't elaborate, but he's in space. Only a gate away, though, so he's probably already made it to one of the stations and is going through processing, with luck," Sasha answered. "I think I may have caught him in the middle of a mission. He mentioned Oliver Solos."

"Solos?" Laurie inquired. "Oliver Solos looking for help from a bounty hunter? That's curious."

"Are you looking for new gossip?" Wolfson asked.

"No, although I might be reaching," the professor admitted. "Solos has his hands in a number of companies, yet none of them have been affected by the curious buy-outs that other companies have faced."

"The ones we've linked to AO?" Sasha asked, his expression thoughtful. "I'm not aware of his entire portfolio, but he does have a stake in both Axiom and Sovereign Arms. You would think both of those would prove to be enticing targets."

"Maybe that's why they've been left alone," the head officer suggested. "Maybe they're too obvious. If they were suddenly bought out or their management replaced out of the blue, even those not looking into a group potentially taking over the world would take notice."

"Maybe they have been," Laurie countered. "We've only looked into public articles. It's not hard to believe they've installed someone behind the scenes or simply buried the story."

The commander nodded, removed his oculars, and rubbed the bridge of his nose. "I'll have to ask for more details once Magellan gets here. Until then, I suggest we go over what we know. I'm sure we'll have a gathering of all parties in a couple of days, so we need to determine where we stand before then."

"Honestly, we're all up to speed—even Wolfson," Laurie

confirmed, twisted in his chair, and hung his legs over the armrests.

"I have to be up to speed," the large man stated. "I have to know what's going on, considering I'll actually be on the field if this all works out."

The professor waved a dismissive hand. "I'll send Cyra in my place—not out of laziness but because she's the better infiltrator. Given the scale of the battle, I'm not much use in the field beyond as an escort. Sasha can attest to that."

The commander shook his head. "You give yourself too little credit, Laurie, but I will agree that it may not be the best place for you. But you realize you'll have to cover our tracks once we all set out."

He frowned but nodded. "Perhaps we can— Oh?" He yanked his tablet from his pocket and glanced at it, a small smile on his lips. "Well, good news. We have new developments. Kaiden finally contacted Chiyo."

"He went dark?" Sasha asked.

"I haven't heard from him since our last talk before he took off," Wolfson revealed. "I wondered what he was up to but he seemed to have had big plans."

"And it seems they bore fruit." Laurie put the tablet on the table between them. The head officer waited curiously while the other man picked it up, read the message, and his eyes widened. "Three hundred? And droids?"

"Three hundred what now?" Wolfson asked.

The professor smiled and placed his chin into the palm of his hand. "Three hundred lovely men and women armed and ready to raid that fortress."

Wolfson's head almost snapped with how fast he turned

to look at him. "What? Where did he get that many recruits?"

"Well, I wouldn't exactly call them 'recruits' considering they are working for spoils," Sasha admitted and handed the tablet to him. "But it appears his previous engagements with gangs has paid some dividends."

The giant took the tablet, read it for himself, and uttered a loud chortle. "Well, damn. It seems the boy may make a good ace by graduation, after all."

"Are you enjoying your new placement?" Dario asked Lycan on the holoscreen as he took a sip of his drink.

"We're getting more action at least, although it's been nothing but bots so far," the brute admitted with a shrug. "I gotta hand it to the brains around here. These droids they are developing may look like the other droids with a nice paint job and new parts, but damn if they aren't a hell of a lot more interesting to crush."

"I promised you that much, didn't I?" The assassin chuckled and took another sip. "And I know what you're thinking. Before you wonder about getting some real action, remember that the whole point of the base is to be a relative secret. It is a registered facility so no flyover by the military should raise any alarms, but that won't stop curious travelers and some less than innocent plunderers from taking a look."

"Like that really needs our special touch," the merc protested, but he also wore an amused grin. "Still, though, we're keeping busy now and this new armor? The fit is fantastic!" He flexed to show off a dark armor set with deep red lines over the arms and chest.

"Only the fit?" Dario questioned, amused. "How about the upgrades? Most would mention that first."

The man waved him off. "I've never been one for more than the necessities, but Jalloh and the others seem to really like them. Speaking of which, Jalloh apologies for not speaking to you personally. He's been busy talking to all the techs and whatnot about security and testing and all that. Personally, I think he's sweet on one of the scientists here. He spends an awful lot of time in the labs and personal rooms if, you catch me."

"Really, now? Well, every man needs his personal distraction. One fights harder when there's something to come back to."

Lycan nodded and studied the assassin. "Talking of fighting, it looks like you're about to head off to take part in some yourself?"

Dario reattached his recharged gauntlet. "Am I that obvious?"

"Are you trying to make me jealous?" the man snickered. "Where are you off to?"

"A personal mission for Merrick—a real one this time. The last one was merely an errand," he admitted, finished his juice, and sighed when he looked at the empty glass. "I always celebrate with a good glass of cognac or wine, but considering where I'm going, I need all my faculties."

"I'm surprised you don't have some mod to take care of inebriation."

He chuckled as he placed the glass down. "That's part of

Kings are with us. Genos and I finished talking to the Azure Halos."

"How did that go?"

"Well enough. We had a small misunderstanding, to begin with but after that, they were almost nice," he admitted.

"What could they bring to the table?" she inquired.

"Fewer hackers than I hoped. They have a decent force, but most of their new recruits are actually engineers. I'm not sure how many we need. They said they have about thirty-something hackers in all but only ten are actually really good."

"If the Halos say they are good, then they are. They are one of the few groups that actually know what that means in the profession," she stated. "On how useful they will be, well, we have a better idea now."

"Have you found out more info from the drive?" He asked.

"Indeed. The building is actually the main fortress in an old military outpost and was refitted by the organization, it looks like," she explained.

That was something, but a building, no matter how big, was less important than what it contained. "Do we have a better idea of the force we'll face?"

"Large. It has a construction division so I'm sure it increases every day," she replied. "What do ours look like?"

"As far as soldiers and all that, we're just shy of three hundred," he answered. "The Halos will also bring in a number of droids of their own, but they aren't in the best place right now on that front. They are building more and the enjoyment. Why would I want something to stop me from having fun?"

The man scratched the back of his head. "Eh, maybe I keep the wrong company. You aug types always seem to want to jam as much new tech in you as possible."

Dario looked at his artificial arms. "These...weren't a personal choice. I'll admit they are quite handy, though. They work well in conjunction with my gauntlets to control— Heh, sorry, I don't mean to bore you." He looked at the screen as an alert scrolled across the monitor to advise him that he was nearing his destination. "I'll have to let you go, for now, Lycan. Once I return, I'll see about getting you something more visceral. Feel free to keep the armor as a token of appreciation."

"I'm happy to." He nodded with a wide smile. "We'll keep this place safe until you get back to us. Go out there and break someone's leg for me, all right?" With that, he signed off.

The assassin smiled. He certainly liked that man's enthusiasm. But as he neared Terra, the first cloud city and home of the World Council, he took a moment to look back at the four golems in the bay of his ship, all of them specially designed to look like four certain people. Four particular council members.

He was there to do more than simply break a leg or two.

CHAPTER NINETEEN

The evening sky hovered over the glowing lights of the Academy plaza. Nearly all the masters were there, talking, laughing, and yelling at one another with excitement and bravado. The tables were as full as ever and in fact, there even seemed to be more Tsuna dishes than normal. Kaiden noticed that more of the human students were brave enough to try them this year as opposed to the hesitation of the last couple of years.

He, however, was not one of them and selected his usual steak, pilaf rice, a baked potato, and grilled asparagus before he carried his tray to the table where all his other friends were already dining and chatting. He took a seat between Chiyo and Genos, glad he'd chosen to take a couple of bottles of beer as well. They would probably be the last he'd have until this was all over. With only a few more days of preparation, he wanted a little relaxation as well. He began cutting into his meal with a smile as he observed the festivities around him and felt the palpable thrill in the spring night air.

"So, how does everyone feel now that there won't be any hand-holding?" Cameron asked and gestured around the table with his fork, specifically at the human ace and marksman. "Kaiden? Flynn? Do you feel any concern now that you won't have the Animus to fix your fuck-ups?"

"The whole point of the Animus is to prepare us for real missions. If we were dying all the time, how would we even be third years by now?" Flynn answered with a laugh and thumped Kaiden on the shoulder. "What's the matter, Kai? Not feeling so sure of yourself?"

"I still have some planning on my end so I won't head out until the end of the week at the earliest," he admitted. "It looks like you might actually win the pot this year."

"You think so, huh?" the bounty hunter asked after he'd swallowed his mouthful of steak. "Luke, Raul, and I have made our plan and it's a masterpiece." He knocked the back of his hand against Raul's shoulder to his left. "Ain't that right?"

"As best as it can be, considering we're going to apprehend a potential terrorist," Raul said as he finished chewing a piece of salmon. "Go ahead and boast about it all you want. Better here than during the mission."

"Terrorist?" Kaiden asked. "How did you get a mission like that?"

"His uncle set it up," Raul explained. "Cameron thought that all the missions the faculty handed out were too… Let's go with not up to his standards."

Cameron speared a piece of asparagus. "Raul is only upset he doesn't have an easy gig, but where's the fun in that? And don't worry about us. This is a simple retrieval.

I've already gone on a dozen missions with my dad and uncle exactly like it."

"You may be prepared for what the mission has to offer," Genos interjected, about to take a bite of a purple orb. "But you should know that's not the only thing you should focus on."

"What are you talking about there, Genos?" Luke asked.

"Well, we are scored not only on completing our mission but how quickly we finish it and in comparison to other students with similar missions," he explained. "I wouldn't put it past some to maybe sabotage others to give them a leg up, like the Death Match. Perhaps not so brazenly, but there could be bugs, invasion drones, or recorders hiding around the plaza," he suggested.

Some of the others began to look around, either with furtive, darting glances or even twisting their whole bodies in search of any tech around them.

"Not to mention potential hacks to your tablets or EIs," Chiyo added.

Izzy looked at her. "Did you find any?"

She shook her head. "No, but it's food for thought."

"I'd rather focus on the food in front of me." Silas chuckled

"Do you really think you should take on a mission that requires such, uh…delicacy?" Otto asked.

Marlo laughed. "You've only known him half as long and you already picked up he's a bit flashy for a bounty hunter, huh?"

"I'm fine," Cameron grumbled and speared another piece of steak. "I have my own way of doing things."

"And we see the effects of it every time you limp out of the Animus pods." Luke snickered.

"Real positive encouragement, teammate."

"Ah, it's only a little tough love, Cam. Positive reinforcement," the titan declared and slapped him jovially on the back. "It's not like I've tried to trade you in or anything."

"Was that an option?" Raul asked and earned a glare from Cameron.

"I wanted to ask how everyone is feeling about tomorrow," Jaxon stated, placed his elbows on the table, and folded his hands. "Does someone have any nervousness or something they would like to discuss before we depart?"

Luke nudged the ace. "Cheer up there, Jax. We've come this far. I think all of us are excited to actually get out in the field—in an official capacity, anyway."

"Does Ramses not count?" Kaiden muttered and took a swig from his bottle.

"He said 'official,'" Mack pointed out. "We had to sneak away at the end with not even a chance to wave at the camera."

"As for any other worries, as much as we should possibly be aware of others trying to get a leg up, I don't think too many will focus on that over their personal plans," Amber interjected.

"Genos can be surprisingly sneaky. You may wanna keep your eye on him," Kaiden said and chuckled.

The Tsuna put his spoon down and tilted his head in mock offense. "I had no plans, only a good-natured joke."

"Kaiden's version of good-natured is suspect," Chiyo said.

The ace held his hands up and grinned. "Hey, I only wanted to lighten him up a little. This is the calm before the storm and all that. We should enjoy it before... Well, the fifty different shades of shit we'll all go through."

"I say bring it!" Mack shouted and pounded his chest. "I'm looking for more action. It's been too quiet for me over the last couple of months."

"Same here," Marlo agreed with a nod. "In fact, the mission Amber, Flynn, and I have will take us all the way to the east coast. We're going after..."

Kaiden smiled as the table began to talk excitedly amongst themselves, discussing their missions, their plans for the final year, what they hoped to accomplish afterward, and where they hoped to go. It made him almost wistful as he recalled the early days and had to admit he was a salty bastard back then.

He thought about the upcoming raid. When he'd got everything in order, he'd felt ready and prepared, but now? There was some hesitation, he had to admit. He wouldn't back down, not a chance in hell, but he had only thought about getting his pound of flesh from these Arbiter bastards. But he realized now that even with all his preparation, he couldn't have a real idea of what to expect or how it would go. He could only see the win. If he wanted to have another moment like this, he would have to focus not only on winning but actually plan for it as well.

A gentle tug on his jacket drew his attention from his thoughts to Chiyo. Either she had similar thoughts or could read his mind. She inclined her head to the edge of the island that overlooked the lake. He nodded and excused himself. Chief disappeared as she followed. There were a few playful catcalls from Izzy, Cameron, and a couple of others but he merely smirked and they ignored their friends.

They leaned on the railing beside one another and gazed at the moonlit waters. "I saw your eyes. Are you worried, Kaiden?"

"I'm only putting things into perspective," he admitted. "I had a message from Wolfson. We'll meet tomorrow. I have the gang leaders' contacts and they'll join us via holoscreen."

"That will help to put things into further perspective." It sounded like an attempt at a joke, albeit half-hearted. "I suppose… No, do not worry. I am prepared."

"You don't need to worry about being a little cautious," he reasoned and leaned forward, his hands tight on the railing. "This is the first real mission we've gone on where there are so many factors we can't possibly see them all. And not everything will be under our control, either."

"Who do you think will lead the charge?" she asked.

Kaiden shrugged. "I want to, but I don't have the leadership skills of Sasha or Wolfson. Hell, maybe even the gang leaders would beat me in that area when it comes to a big force like that. But I'll lead the literal charge, in any case."

"I see." She nodded. "Be careful, okay?"

He chuckled. "You should have known what you signed up for when—" He broke off when he noticed her faraway stare and despondent expression. His smile faded and he reached a hand out to turn her head gently and rest his forehead against her own. "We'll make it out of this, all right? I promise."

"I know," she agreed but avoided his gaze slightly.

"Promise me the same," he stated.

She looked at him, surprised at first, but determination filled her eyes. "I promise."

They remained close to one another in companionable silence under the stars and shared a last moment of peace and serenity before they set off to battle.

CHAPTER TWENTY

When the sun rose on the morning after the feast, there were already many master students on the grounds, most rushing to the carrier station to head into town. Some had ships waiting in the docks, either rented or gifts from well-to-do parents of aspiring pilots. Kaiden, along with Genos and Chiyo, was among the throngs, but they were not setting out. They came to say farewell and wish their friends luck. Cameron, Raul, Luke, Flynn, Marlo, and Amber were all leaving early.

"I'm surprised you're not heading out already," Kaiden whispered to Jaxon as they watched the six board the carriers into town.

"I could say the same to you," the Tsuna responded and clasped both behind his back. "It's a rather large mission you've undertaken, correct?"

"Do you think I would go small at this point?" He chuckled. "I think they'd dock me points if that was the case."

"Same with me." Jaxon glanced at Genos, who had moved closer to the windows of the carrier to watch his friends leave. "He is going with you?"

He nodded and watched with amusement when Genos leapt up to wave to the team on the upper deck. "He insisted."

"I am aware. Take care of him. I'll be sure we finish our mission quickly so we can all come back and celebrate."

"We'll meet you back here." He offered a hand and the two friends shook. "I look forward to it."

He nodded and called Silas and Izzy to join him before they walked to the Animus Center for a little more training before they headed off on their mission.

Genos and Chiyo wandered over and the ace checked his HUD. "It looks like they're ready," he said and his friends nodded in return. "Let's join them."

The trio walked into Laurie's office. The professor was there, obviously, along with Wolfson and Sasha. Kaiden smiled when Magellan, in his wide-brimmed hat and dark armored jacket, greeted him with a wave.

"It's good to see you again, Kaiden." He stood and walked over to clap him heartily on the back. "It's been a while."

"It really has." He returned the back-slapping gesture. "It's good to see you in one piece still, but I guess that's why you earned those three stars, huh?"

"It'll probably be four stars soon." He laughed and removed his hat to reveal a bandanna beneath, then spun the hat in his hand. "I'd ask what you've been up to but the commander has filled me in and...well, I guess with all of us here, it's fairly obvious now."

"I guess so." The ace looked around. "But we still have some details to hammer out."

"Indeed." Laurie nodded and placed an EI pad on the floor between the group. "We're ready to begin. If you can get the leaders on the line, I'll try to get Cyra—oh, never mind."

The door behind them opened and the infiltrator entered. "Sorry, I was delayed helping some of the guys in security."

"It's all good," Kaiden said and brought up the contacts on his tablet. "We still need to get the others on the line. I sent them a message last night, so they should be ready."

It took only a few minutes for Zena, Desmond, Janis, Fritz, and Kit to appear on Laurie's holoscreens. They all looked around the room and the leaders of the Riders and Kings seemed surprised to see the leaders of the Halos as the hacker gang was to see almost everybody.

"Is that Alexander Laurie?" Janis asked.

"I prefer Professor Laurie but I suppose you aren't a student." He chortled. "And I can give you a pass. After all, you are helping tremendously."

"Yes, of course," the man said with a small bow.

"You should have told us you were working with him in the first place, Kaiden." Fritz chuckled. "Janis is a huge fanboy of Laurie."

The Halos leader looked like he wanted to tell his team-mate to shut up but simply shrugged.

"Not to mention Commanders Sasha Chevalier and

Baioh Wolfson," Desmond said with open admiration. "I guess this isn't some foolhardy plan by some simple merc, huh?"

"Is that what you thought it was?" Kaiden sighed and looked at the men who had been mentioned. "If I had known you had such big fan clubs, I would have parlayed with that."

"You did quite well without relying on our names," the commander stated. "That deserves its own praise."

"We should get to it, then," Magellan interjected. The gang leaders immediately recognized him.

"Is that—" Desmond began before he was cut off by Wolfson.

"Enough with the prattle. We can share stories and take selfies later after the battle," he snarked and folded his arms. "Laurie will fill you in on what we know. We need to make a plan and get going as quickly as we can. So you need to know that there are no stupid questions and listen closely."

Laurie, Wolfson, and Sasha filled the leaders in on the current layout of the fortress. Kaiden considered all the details as they explained the layout and what kind of forces they could expect to face. The other side undoubtedly had significant numbers. Kit explained that they had a force of about two hundred and twenty droids—no doubt more than they planned to provide before they knew everyone involved, but Kaiden wouldn't complain. If them being starstruck meant they would go all out, that was a bonus.

The fortress, however, according to the information on the device, mustered forces of about three hundred and fifty droids and a hundred security personnel. No doubt that had strengthened in the months since. The best-case scenario was that the droids had doubled and the security force remained relatively the same. Still, it was better to plan to face one thousand—an over-estimate was preferable to an under-estimate.

"We can't give them time to rally all their troops to attack us as one," Sasha stated. "We need to keep the pressure on and find a way to reduce numbers quickly."

"We can handle that," Desmond vowed. "We're the Skyway Kings. I told Kaiden that this division has more ground forces than usual, but we still have the rep for our aerial combatants. On top of that, we have our own fleet of fighters. They've been gathering dust for the most part, but I had our engineers make them clean and shiny again for the last mission before he approached us. That means we can hammer them from above—they don't have much of an air force, right?"

"Not from what we've discovered, but they do have a considerable number of anti-air missiles and cannons," Laurie pointed out.

"Those should be the first things we target, then," Zena stated firmly. "We need to eliminate those, cover our backs when they send in the waves of droids, and once we clear out a good number of them, Desmond and his boys can do their thing."

"Our hackers can probably remotely disable a good number as well," Kit added. "Our engineers are also outfitted with nano grenades. They've been working on a batch since Kaiden paid us a visit."

"I'm glad to inspire when I can." He chuckled and jerked his thumb toward Genos. "Although those were his nanos."

"We were able to engineer a few using nanos scattered around the cannons," Fritz explained.

"Some must have been fried from the residual electricity of the cannons," Genos muttered and tapped his infuser. "I need to make a note of that."

"Kaiden said the hackers will focus on trying to take the system over," Janis recalled. "For that, we need to get into the heart of the base. As Kit said, I'm sure there are things we can do remotely, but this battle will last much longer and be far bloodier if we can't get in."

"You'll be with Chiyo and Cyra," Kaiden said and pointed at the women. "They are the best infiltrators in the academy, and that's not hyperbole."

"We'll give you your opening," Wolfson promised. "As much as we'd like to simply drop you on the roof and let you make your way in, that seems like it would lead to some—"

"Is that an option?" Chiyo asked. Everyone turned to look at her. "Not all of us, obviously, but a small force. We can go through and take over interior defenses. It would make it easier for the main force to enter when the time comes."

"That's…not a bad idea there, lass," the head officer said and stroked his chin thoughtfully as he looked at Sasha. "It might also split the defense force. As long as the infiltrators keep to hit-and-run tactics, they won't have to worry about being overwhelmed."

Sasha thought it over and asked Janis, "How many hackers do you have who are comfortable in the field?"

"I would say about twelve, but that's Kit's division."

She nodded and took out a tablet. "While I would agree that we have twelve field operatives for an attack like that, I would say eight would be better, along with myself. I can also bring some droids and a few engineers to help if that's all right with you, Fritz."

"Take them," he agreed quickly.

"I'll send some of my raiders to back you up," Zena offered. "They handle heavy weapons but they are quick and they'll be helpful if you get caught."

"I'll join you," Magellan stated and placed a fist across his chest. "I'll help you get inside and if things go peachy, I'll have a perch to snipe from as well."

Sasha nodded. "Then Chiyo, Cyra, Kit, and Magellan will be the leads on that front. Keep us informed as you make progress." He looked around the room. "The rest of us will be on the ground. I take it everyone is stocked?"

"Of course!" Desmond boasted. "You can't run a proper gang without the proper equipment."

"I'm actually going to see Julio again," Kaiden advised them. "He said he might have something for us."

"Knowing him, it'll be top quality and that will be an even bigger help." The commander addressed Zena and Desmond. "We won't have enough for everyone, I'm sure, so send me a list of your best people and their specialties. I'll distribute the weapons and gear once Kaiden gives me the list."

"Understood," Zena agreed.

"Got it, sir," Desmond replied.

"Transport," Laurie said. "Is everyone good on that front as well?"

"It'll be tight but we should be good," Fritz confirmed.

"Same here," Zena concurred.

"I have some spare ships I bought at auction," Wolfson offered. "I plan to make them into security vessels, but we can spread the troops around better with extra ships."

Sasha nodded. "Have them ready, Wolfson."

"Aye, I'm on it."

"I guess all we need is a date, then," Magellan said finally.

"This Saturday. We'll meet on the battlefield in the morning," Sasha stated. "Can everyone be ready by then?"

"I'll go see Julio right after this," Kaiden promised. "I'll get the list and see what he's offering."

"We'll have the droids ready," Janis assured everyone.

"And we'll be ready as well." Zena looked at Desmond, who nodded.

"I'll send you the coordinates tomorrow," the commander continued. "I'll honor everything Kaiden has promised you. But know that we are doing this as much for the world as we are for ourselves."

"Everyone has a stake," the Kings' leader agreed. "We'll turn them to dust—everything but the expensive stuff, at least."

"Does anyone wanna make a bet on how this will go?" Fritz asked and earned an irate glare from Janis and Kit.

"I bet my Riders will have the highest kill count." Zena sounded confident.

"Hah! Not with my Kings in their domain," Desmond retorted.

"We have enough droids now to equal both your forces combined," Fritz challenged.

As the leaders argued amongst themselves, Laurie leaned over to Cyra and Wolfson to speak. Kaiden looked at Sasha to indicate that he would leave. The commander nodded and the ace Kaiden rested a hand on the shoulders of his teammates before he headed off to see Julio.

The battle would be upon them soon.

CHAPTER TWENTY-ONE

K aiden pushed open the doors to the Emerald Lounge and they closed behind him with a muted click. It was dark inside and quiet, too, with no customers or Julio in sight. The bar was dimly lit and he immediately grew concerned. He had told his friend he was coming, and the proprietor said he had something to show him and the door would be open. Where the hell was he?

He took a few more steps into the room and a message flashed in his HUD

Ready for you downstairs. In the vault.

Julio's secret stash was stored below so he was probably taking inventory. Which was perfect, as that was what he'd come for. He made his way past the bar to the office door in the back of the lounge. When he entered, he turned to the painting of Logan Lopez's *Mujer de Los Muertos* and pressed a switch below the frame. A piece of the wall slid up and he descended the stairs behind it.

When he reached the bottom, his jaw dropped. The vault was open and even from the entrance, he could see it was way more stocked than he remembered with guns, blades, explosives, medical supplies, and new racks of armor sets. The barkeep and broker had been very busy these last few days—maybe even before they set this whole thing off.

"There you are, Kaiden." He turned and the other man waved at him once he placed a small crate on top of a stack of six. Julio wore armor himself, seemingly breaking it in because he twisted his arms around as if they were a little stiff.

"Should I ask how you got all this or is it in my best interest not to?" he asked with a chuckle and traced his fingers over a shotgun. He didn't know the model and it seemed to be at least a decade old, but it shone like new.

"Considering you and your friends will be using it all, I think that would be a worse offense than simply being privy to where they came from," his friend retorted as he approached. He stopped a couple of feet in front of him and gestured to the suit he wore. "What do you think?"

The armor was mostly black but some kind of red mesh-like material around the ribs, elbow, and knees resembled micro chainmail. It looked easier to move around in than heavy and medium armor and much more breathable too. "It looks good," the ace confirmed. "Do you need protection for your next fling?"

Julio smiled, picked up the shotgun he had looked at, and held it in both hands across his chest. "I need protection for the fight we're heading to."

"We're?" he asked and emphasized the word. "You want to come along?"

The man's smile dropped and was replaced by firm determination. "Of course. I'm not missing this."

Kaiden leaned against one of the tables. "I thought the whole reason you bought this place was to give up that kind of thing." He looked around at the weaponry. "Well, give up doing it yourself."

His companion leaned back against a table opposite him. "I gave up doing shake-downs, collection work, and the day to day bullshit that wears you down after a while. I might not be in the gang anymore, but I won't give up helping another Dead-Eye when something big goes down."

The ace placed his hand over his Dead-Eye tattoo and gave that some thought. "You can't really leave it behind, can you?"

Julio tapped his arm where his own tattoo was. "You haven't been in contact with your old friends since coming here, but if one of them called you and said they needed help, would you go?"

"Of course." He nodded.

"It seems you can't give it up either. There's your answer."

He straightened and proffered his hand. "Thanks, Julio."

Their handshake was firm, one of friends and mutual respect. "Of course, Kaiden." The proprietor turned and placed the shotgun behind him. "Now that all the sentimental stuff is out of the way, what do you think of the goods?"

"I think you did a damn fine job." Kaiden admired the entire room full of equipment and a thought came to him. "One thing, though."

"What's that?"

He looked at him with a befuddled frown. "How will we move all this?"

Julio chuckled and shrugged. "I kind of hoped you could bring some friends to help with that."

He nodded and retrieved his tablet. "I guess I should give Zena and Desmond another call. They probably won't be too mad once we tell them what we have."

Chiyo, Genos, and Cyra looked out over the lake. All three simply took a moment to admire the view, but Genos was eventually the first to break the silence. "Are either of you worried?"

Neither responded immediately. Cyra looked like she was trying to shake her head, but it stopped mid-swing. Chiyo clutched the railing and looked down. "This will be tough, but we are all used to that," she began and turned to focus on her companions. "We have a plan, forces, and each other. That should make us fight harder than we ever have before."

"I feel guilty that we cannot tell the others," the Tsuna admitted and his hand fiddled with his infuser. "Kin Jaxon leaves tomorrow. He believes we are still going on an escort and retrieval mission for the professor."

"Speaking of which, I already have the item that we are supposed to 'retrieve' waiting in my office," Cyra said before she realized that she had interrupted. "I'm sorry."

"No, it's all right. Thank you, friend Cyra."

"Friend already?" she asked with a giggle. "You are fast to make friends."

"You are friends with Chiyo, yes?" he asked. "Then you are mine as well if you would like to be."

"I certainly would." She nodded and smiled before she turned to look at the lake once again. "I remember the first time… Not to be morose, but the first time I went on a mission where I was sure there would be casualties."

Chiyo nodded and spoke softly. "I'm sure everyone will give it their all. But we haven't participated in a battle like this, at least outside the Animus. They have the numbers and technological advantage."

"Their position is strong as well," Genos added.

She nodded, silent for a moment before she continued. "Even if we all perform flawlessly, there's too much we can't plan for or anticipate, and there will be those who fall. All we can do is look out for each other and make sure that number is as low as can be."

Cyra straightened and drew a deep breath. "And make sure that number is as large as can be for our adversaries."

Chiyo nodded. "We'll both be in charge of the hacker team. I'll make sure to have your back."

"And I'll do the same," the other woman agreed. "And we'll make sure the world knows about these creeps."

Genos, caught in the middle, looked from one to the other before he backed away and placed a hand on his chest and two fingers in the air, his normal salute. "He may not be here currently, but I believe I can speak for friend Kaiden and myself and say that we will make sure to hold the line."

The women nodded to him and as one, their gazes

drifted to the Animus Center. "Only a couple of days until we set out," Cyra noted. "Do you care to squeeze in a little more training?"

Her companions looked at each other. "Let's go," Chiyo agreed and the trio made their way over to the Center with determined strides.

CHAPTER TWENTY-TWO

That Friday morning, the second and first years began to take their finals. The fourth years had left for theirs around the same time as the masters had. The Academy felt almost deserted after the initial breakfast rush of students who hastily scarfed their food and departed. Kaiden assumed it was like this every year, but he'd never really paid attention. Now, though, as he strolled through the plaza, the emptiness really struck him. He would win—they would win, he was somehow sure of that—but the feeling of morbid concern hovered over him. None of his friends were there to see him off as all had already left. He checked his messages to find one from Chiyo, Genos, Cyra, and even Magellan, all informing him they were ready and heading to the ships.

He took another look at the Academy buildings and the soldiers' dorm in the distance, and the feeling wouldn't leave him.

"Hey, boyo." Wolfson strode toward him—he must have really been out of it because it wasn't like the officer was the quietest man—and stopped only a couple of feet in front of him. He wore a shirt with the Nexus Academy logo on it and dark pants. "Your teammates have been training while you were away. Sasha and I have made preparations. It wasn't until last night that Zena told us you stayed with them."

Kaiden nodded and held his hands up to show red lines and bruises. "Julio came through damn well but I had a ton of shit to move and prepare myself. Even with the Riders' help, it took way longer than we thought."

The man smiled, a little more at ease now that he knew he had been out doing something rather than let the tension get to him. "We'll leave tonight and be at the stronghold by dawn tomorrow."

"That quick?" he asked. "What kind of jets do you have on those ships?"

"The kind that takes you a third of the way across the world in twelve hours," the man retorted. "Zena was already sending teams over, wasn't she?"

He nodded and slid his hands into his pockets. "Yeah, but they were recon and setup teams. The rest—"

"They'll be leaving soon, I know," his companion interrupted, folded his arms, and took a deep breath. "I'm making sure you do."

The ace frowned and leveled him with a challenging stare. "Do you really think I'm not taking this seriously, Wolfson? I know what's at stake and what I'm asking everyone to do—to potentially give up if this goes wrong."

"What you're asking, eh?" the giant muttered and stroked his beard. "That's what I was looking for."

Kaiden blinked and wracked his brain in an effort to determine what he was talking about. "Looking for?"

"I told you we all had skin in the game, didn't I?" Wolfson returned his glare. "You're piling all this on yourself now, aren't you?"

He shrugged and began to walk away. "I'm the one who gathered everybody, aren't I? Sasha and Laurie have been apprehensive since the start. If anyone is making a move it's because of me."

"I guess it's become a little more real for you now, hasn't it, Kaiden?" he called and the ace stopped in his tracks. "I know you're not getting cold feet. But trying to take all that responsibility and put it on you... That won't be good when the bodies start dropping."

Kaiden tensed when he saw images of the worst-case scenario playing in his head. He shook them off and looked over his shoulder. "I assume you speak from experience?"

Wolfson closed his eye. It could have been sarcastic, but he'd picked up the tone that indicated a genuine question. He nodded. "Aye, and if you let that feeling eat at you long enough, that's worse than any death I've seen." He opened his eye to look at him again, but this look was more concerned than zealous. "Everyone is here by choice, even if it's only incentive on the gangs' part. We all know what's at stake. It is virtuous that you aren't simply writing them off as expendable. I've known men like that." His voice turned to a growl with that statement. "But if we are to succeed—if you wanna live to see it—focus on the fighting. It's what you're good at. You've brought all of us together, sure, now lead by example."

He turned around, his stance relaxed a little, and he managed a smile. "I'm that easy to read, huh?"

"I've seen a lot." The large man folded his arms again and regarded him steadily. "I've told you before that I'm no psychologist, but I know with only a glance when a man needs help to stay on his feet."

The ace chuckled, nodded, and waved for him to join him. "Let's go double-check the inventory and make sure we have everything."

Wolfson nodded and they walked on together. "I was on my way to do that myself."

"I assumed as much. Always be sure you're prepared, or you'll be sure that you're fucked."

The officer laughed and it seemed to echo around the island. "So some of my wisdom has rubbed off, eh?"

He merely shrugged as they walked down the steps to the docks. "Yeah, 'wisdom.'"

Jalloh stood on the roof of the tower, his gazed fixed on the lights below. It was a very pretty sight, albeit somewhat mechanical—which was appropriate, considering where they were. Rows of small buildings, all about twenty-five feet tall, resembled cubes of black metal and glowstrips lined the pathways between so the few humans who were stationed here could find their way. Each building held supplies, parts, and defective models in storage, waiting for repair. All of them were specifically created for the purposes of his employers. He hadn't been told much, but even a fool could tell they were planning for something big

—maybe even to take on the council. Hopefully, his team had been recruited by the winning side.

The door to the roof opened and Lycan stepped out. He yawned before he finished a bottle of beer and seemed ready to throw it carelessly aside before he noticed his leader. Sheepishly, he slid it into his pocket for later disposal.

"Hey, Jalloh, what are you doing up here?"

"Merely observing," he replied and returned his attention to the scene sprawled below. "It's rather mystifying, isn't it?"

His teammate followed his gaze as he took a fresh bottle from a container he held. "Honestly, the layout looks like those motherboards from the early twenty-first century." He held the container up to offer him a beer, but he declined. The large man shrugged and removed the top before he took a few swallows. "You said you were here observing, Have you seen anything good?"

The merc leader put his hand against the railing. "The night sky and the dancing lights below, but I assume none of that would interest you, huh?"

"I can get in touch with my feelings on occasion," Lycan retorted. "I'm surprised you've kept us on this gig so long, even with as patient as you are. You have to be bored by now, right?"

"This is an occasion where I'll wait to see things play out," Jalloh stated. "I believe that things could turn dramatic quite soon."

"How so?"

"That's what I'm waiting to find out." He patted the large man on the shoulder and turned to walk away. "Don't worry, Lycan. I'm sure we can find you some excitement in the not too distant future."

His response seemed somewhere between a sigh and hearty chuckle. "I hope so. They don't get beer shipments that often here and I'm almost out." He finished the second beer, retrieved the first bottle, and placed both empties into the container before he withdrew a third. With a grimace, he raised it in a mock toast to the night sky and hoped he would have some action. It seemed like something to drink to.

CHAPTER TWENTY-THREE

"Get it together, boy. They'll be here any minute," Wolfson shouted as he bounded off the ramp to the ship.

Kaiden huffed as he charged up the ramp with one of the last cases and yelled a response. "I've moved fifteen more crates than you have. Why are you crying instead of working?"

"Mine were bigger." The giant wandered over to a long, dark box nearby.

"This is about quantity, not quality, big man," the ace retorted and his voice echoed inside the ship as he placed his load down and turned to retrieve another. "Don't you need to get suited up anyway?"

The head officer pressed a button on the side of the case to open it and reveal a suit of red armor. "That's what I'm doing. Where the hell is your loadout?"

"Julio is bringing it, along with Genos' and Chiyo's," he responded as he picked up another case.

"Your gig dealer?" Wolfson stripped his shirt off and

picked up the armor underlay. "I guess he's also your outfitter too, huh? He's playing it close, isn't he?"

"He's bringing it because he's going with us," Kaiden explained. "I can't bring full armored apparel into the school. You should know that as head of security."

"Julio is coming?" The man actually looked startled. "As in to fight as well?"

"Yep, it shocked me too." He placed the last of the crates into the bay and sauntered down the ramp. "Throw me the card to the armory. I need to grab my pistol."

"I brought Debonair with me. It's in that bag over there." The man gestured behind him as he zipped the underlay and began donning the chest and arms of his suit.

"I mean the zapper," Kaiden replied but checked the bag anyway and removed Debonair.

"The shock pistol? What do you want that for? You know it's mostly a showpiece. Hell, you barely carry it around now."

"I'll take all the advantages I can," he responded and helped his instructor lock the back of his suit. "Besides, we're mostly fighting droids, right? A full charge at close range should disrupt their systems." He watched for a moment as his mentor began putting on the leg plates, noted the individual pieces, and sighed. "I noticed the new armor and hoped it was…you know, actually new."

"This was the latest set when I left the military," Wolfson explained. "They don't make them like this anymore. It has low shielding, but the plating, heat reinforced interior, and disruption lining is something beautiful. It would take a hail of lasers to actually cut through this stuff."

"That…actually sounds nice," he admitted. "Why did they stop making it?"

"Convenience and price." The head officer pulled on one of his gauntlets. "I'll admit that this armor was already a few years old when I got it. By then, shielding had become more common and practical and batteries became easier to carry and could recharge the shielding faster. This armor can take a beating, but once it's damaged, you'll pay a hefty price to repair it. Or the WC will if you were in the military like I was."

"Ah, that makes sense." The ace nodded and retrieved his tablet. "I'll contact Zena to see how the first team is doing. I've received no messages so either they are fine and trying to lay low or we should probably expect some shit on the way."

"Good call. I'll be ready soon and I'll check to see what's taking Sasha so long." Wolfson locked his left boot in place.

Kaiden opened his contacts, selected Zena, and waited for a connection.

"This is Zena," the Fire Riders' leader answered and motioned for two grunts to move out of her way as she walked into the tent. "What do you need, Kaiden?"

"I'm only checking to see how everything is going," he replied. "We're about to leave and will be there in the morning, but we'll go directly into the fight. I wanted to see if everything is going well with you so far."

"It's peachy, really." She sighed. "I'm only being some-what sarcastic. The Halos got here around the same time I did. Kit and Fritz have patrolled and found several types of sensor and camera equipment. I'm actually quite glad they came along. My kids are good soldiers but not the most cautious kind. They would probably have stumbled right into them."

"So you haven't been detected?" he asked.

She shook her head. "No. Kit has made sure we're safely hidden from normal surveillance while Fritz is still out in the forest looking for more equipment, but we should be good until the push. After that, I guess it won't matter too much if they see us."

"They'll certainly know we're there when it starts," he agreed. "Did Kit bring any droids with her?"

"Some—a few dozen—but we've kept them deactivated for now. A group of droids suddenly appearing in the forest would be easy to pick up and more than a little suspicious," she explained. "Janis is bringing the rest on larger ships—modified Zeppelins, from my understanding. Desmond will bring the remainder of our forces alongside you."

"All right. We'll start the fight and keep them busy while you get your troops and the droids ready."

"Understood." She nodded and glanced back when a noise caught her attention. "Hold on a moment, Kaiden. Kit wants to talk."

"I guess we never got around to talking about compensation for her jet bike," he muttered. "Right, put her on."

The Azure Halo lieutenant took the tablet. "Kaiden, Fritz sent some photos. He's run into some of the droids."

"Was there any fighting?"

She frowned. "I wouldn't be so calm if it came to that. He's only scouting right now but take a look."

The photos showed humanoid droids with white faces and slits for eyes and mouths. Kaiden zoomed in on the eyes. No lights were visible, but he could faintly see what looked like cameras. They were well armored and even the exposed sections seemed to be reinforced. "I've never seen ones like these before," he admitted. "They look almost like Havoc droids, but I don't see any weapons. I assume the arms change into cannons or something, right?"

"Flip over a few photos," she told him.

He scrolled down and paused at the image that displayed the mechanicals ripping metal objects apart. One showed a droid holding an arm out with a blue light emitting from it. "Shit. These are probably based on the one I fought back at y'alls base."

"I reached the same conclusion," she stated. "For mass production, I'm sure some of the finer details were left on the floor but fighting a horde of those things will be quite difficult."

"Do you think it could hurt the bottom line?" he asked. "Maybe I'm hopeful, but when we estimated the number of bots they had, we assumed they would only use modified droid designs, which would have been faster."

"They might have less. From the pictures Fritz sent, this seems to be the bulk of their force," she confirmed. "But did you notice the guards amongst the pics?"

The ace refocused on the images and identified men and women in medium and light armor. There were only a few but it confirmed a human presence there. "The armor doesn't look like anything special. It's certainly not off the rack but it doesn't look like something they made themselves."

"I'm sure they are modified," Kit reasoned. "But you also said this organization has hands in several companies you know of. It's certainly feasible that this armor was made by one of them to their specifications."

"Yeah. It certainly could be," he murmured. "I guess we'll have a ton of things to look into once we pick it off the bodies."

"That would be the most direct way," she agreed. "I'll let you go now. See you in the morning—assuming we can find each other."

"Are you still heading up part of the hacker team?" he asked.

"Fritz and I will work with a group of hackers and engineers before we break off. I'll then head into the main building from the ground. Your infiltrators will have to take care of the airdrop, but don't worry. Janis will send a team to meet them there."

"All right. Best of luck."

"Same to you." With that, she signed off. Kaiden put the tablet away as Wolfson walked up to him, a large shotgun with a rotating chamber slung over his shoulder. As he gave him a wide grin, the door to the warehouse opened and Sasha, Magellan, Cyra, Genos, and Chiyo walked in. Behind them, Julio pushed a cart with several crates.

The ace nodded a greeting as he approached them. "It's good to see you. Wolfson and I readied the ships." He gestured to the three aircraft behind him. "We'll meet up with Desmond to pick up some of the troops and we'll all set off together. The ground forces are ready at the base."

"And Janis?" Sasha asked.

"He's flying in as well with the majority of the droid infantry."

"It looks like you have everything set to go, Kaiden," Magellan commented and slung his rifle over his shoulder. "Are we ready?"

"Almost." He studied the armored Magellan, Sasha, Julio, and Cyra. "You guys only need to get on the ships."

CHAPTER TWENTY-FOUR

K aiden sat on the bench as a couple of Desmond's troops checked one another's gear. Jet-jocks was the slang term for these outfits—light armor, large packs on their backs, mods for stabilizing, and weighted segments on their gear to help to remain level during flight. Something always seemed a little off with the equipment, even in the professional outfits. The Skyway Kings, while they certainly had a reputation, were not so professional. He could smell the leaks in the gear and he closed any external vents in his helmet and relied on the meager oxygen tank. It definitely wouldn't help to get high on the fumes and on that note, he also checked his weapons to make sure they weren't sparking. He would also prefer not to die in an explosion before they even reached the big fight.

It would be a rather stupid epitaph—charrr-poof.

He was distracted by one of the few dozen ground troops the Fire Riders had left behind from the first group. The man rolled something around in his gauntlet—a rosary by the looks of it, although the beads were made of glass and the various symbols seeming handcrafted from junk and scraps.

"Are you religious?" the ace asked.

The man looked up. He wore a rounded helmet with a faded visor and while it looked in shape, the repairs were rough. "I am for the next day or two," he responded.

"Have you made many confessions before heading off?" he asked with a chuckle.

"Yeah." The merc continued to turn the fetish in his large hands as if by rote. "Although honestly, I hope to get enough off the haul when we win this thing to pay for a big-ass penitence."

"Do you wanna toss a couple of creds into the swear jar?" he joked.

The man laughed weakly but honestly. "That's an ongoing tab."

Kaiden and glanced at Genos, who now made his way through a few of the other soldiers toward him. "Wolfson wanted me to tell you we're almost there," the Tsuna stated.

The Fire Rider nodded, stowed his rosary, and picked up his machine gun before he moved to the back of the ship to join the other 'shock troopers'—or, at least, that's what they were today. The ace moved back to allow the jockeys to take their positions at the door and then made his way over to the cockpit.

He placed a hand on Wolfson's shoulder and leaned closer to the monitor on the screen. It displayed five different panels with Sasha, Magellan, Desmond, Julio, and Zena on each. "Is everyone ready?"

"It would be a hell of a time to get worried now."

Magellan chuckled. "I'll peel off and take a couple of Desmond's fighters with me to make sure the hackers get on that roof and escort them where they need to go."

"Thank you, Magellan," he replied and drew in a sharp breath. "Can you tell Chiyo something?"

"Good luck?" the bounty hunter guessed. "She wished you the same. She also wanted me to pass along that you need to focus on what you do best and she'll do the same—saving your ass."

He chuckled. "She's a little cocky, ain't she? But that's about right."

"I'll make sure it all goes right, I promise." Magellan glanced to the side at another screen. "There aren't any turrets we need to worry about, right?"

"There were but there are less now," Kit confirmed. "Fritz took care of the bigger ones last night, but I should let you all know it won't be a permanent fix once they realize they are offline."

"And about how long will that be?" Julio questioned.

"About the time they try firing them and they don't work," Fritz answered as he appeared on a new screen and turned the monitor into two columns of three panels. "I would guess you'll have a few minutes of relative safety but the smaller turrets are still active, so fly like you don't wanna crash."

"That's generally the basics," Julio retorted. "I'll try to take out what I can with my cannons once I drop my cargo."

"How long can you last?" Zena asked.

He shrugged. "As long as my baby will hold."

"I hope you work fast or that ship is well-shielded," Fritz commented.

"I'll help you with that, Julio," Wolfson assured him. "Along with the jockeys and fighters. We'll take care of the problem before it becomes one."

"Janis arrived only a few hours ago," Kit informed them. "The droids are ready to go. He's already set up and will begin their activation soon."

"We're on the move as well," Zena stated. "You'll probably still beat us to the gate by a few minutes, at least."

"Arrive fashionably." Kaiden looked up as Magellan banked away. Three fighter ships followed and Wolfson pulled ahead. The ace took one last look at the monitor. "Keep a kill count, everyone, and let's compare when this is over." Somehow, the flashback silliness of their student training made him feel a little better like they would all actually be there to compare at the end.

Lycan yawned loudly and stretched his massive arms above his head as the morning sun crept over the mountains behind the base. He was dressed in nothing but a pair of black briefs and he let the wind tease at him while he smiled a toothy grin to meet the day. His morning stretches—one of the few routines he'd kept as a strict tradition ever since he was in the Omega Horde and one of his favorite parts of the normal day. He had even been able to persuade some of the other soldiers to join him, although he could see they didn't seem to share his enthusiasm for the tradition. As fighters, they should know the importance of keeping limber.

"Uh, Mr Lycan, sir," one of them called and pointed to the side. "Your tablet is blinking."

He frowned and glanced at the device. It could only be Raz. Both Jalloh and Cascina were well-mannered enough not to interrupt him in the mornings. He scowled as he picked it up and, sure enough, it was the team hacker. "What is it, Raz?" His tone was deliberately curt when he answered the call and his teammate's face appeared onscreen.

"Lycan, tell me what you see," Raz demanded. His voice sounded anxious and his expression seemed doubly so.

"A little bastard ruining the beginning of my day," he retorted.

"No, idiot!" he snapped. "Look at the horizon. I'm getting a ton of readings here."

"What?" Lycan muttered and looked over his shoulder. "Are you sure that's not another surge from the core?"

"Everyone in here is reading the same thing," the hacker explained feverishly. "One second, it was fine and in the next, there was a giant—"

"Hold on." He held up a hand and turned to squint at the horizon. Several dots showed against the sky. As they drew closer, more appeared, followed by a couple more after a second or two. And, he realized, they were getting bigger. The familiar sound of fighter engines edged into the silence.

Part of him was worried but the other was simply excited. Finally, something was happening. But as more dots appeared and some turned into actual shapes that now raced toward the base, he realized that a whole ton of something was happening all at once.

"Son of a bitch!" he cried and startled the other guards. "We're under attack."

No sooner had he yelled the warning before a barrage of fire sent everyone on the roof into a scramble to find cover. Below, the droids responded with the comforting clank of metal against metal. Lycan turned to one of the defensive cannons but it hadn't moved. "Raz! The cannons."

"They aren't responding," his teammate stated. "Someone hid a series of junk commands in the systems. I need to force them out."

"Reboot them, you jackass."

"That would take longer," the hacker countered. "I'll do what I know, and you do what you know. Go kill them!"

Lycan snorted and noted that the other guards were already bolting for the door to head to the armory. "I'll ignore the disrespectful tone," he muttered and tossed the tablet aside as he walked to the stairway. "Because I can take my anger out on something else now."

The last of the jockeys leapt out and Kaiden caught hold of a railing above him when Wolfson plummeted to a lower altitude and slowed barely enough as the back of the ship opened. He drew Sire, looked back, and raised an arm. The mixed team of gang members hollered, cheered, and raised their weapons in a show of unity and he pointed and led them forward. He was the first to jump and the shocks in his armor dampened the impact when he landed and whipped around to see the jockeys had already begun to cause enough chaos to draw the droids' attention.

The ace charged a shot as one of the mechanicals focused on him. It's arm transformed into a cannon but before it could even aim it toward him, he fired and it took the almost fully charged shot full in the chest. Unfortunately, it didn't buckle or break. While it fell back a little, it regained its balance and he was caught momentarily off guard and tried hastily to charge another shot. Laser fire and kinetic rounds erupted around him to obliterate the droid and a few of the others in a hail of deadly projectiles. This was immediately followed by more raucous shouts and whoops as the soldiers who landed behind him surged forward. Some screamed for loot while others argued who had achieved those kills.

A group of droids exited one of the buildings—a warehouse or assembly building if he had to guess. He turned his weapon to them and fired, but having learned from the last shot, he followed quickly with a thermal. The droids exploded twice over and he barreled after his team while a fighter ship screamed over him.

The raid had begun.

CHAPTER TWENTY-FIVE

Jalloh and Cascina waited for the doors to the main building to open. Raz was busy dealing with the internal security measures and unraveling the numerous 'small annoyances,' as he put it. The merc leader could hear explosions outside that actually made the building shake. Whoever this was came prepared to fight and cause a ruckus. But, when the doors finally parted and the numerous Arbiter droids at his back entered the battle, he would respond in kind.

"That's one cannon down," Julio yelled as his ship's guns finally dislodged the west cannon. It plummeted to shatter into pieces and destroy the buildings and robots that tried to slow him down with laser fire from over a hundred feet below.

"Well done," Sasha complimented him and tapped a few

buttons on his ship's console. "I'll connect my ship's autopilot to yours. I need to get on the ground."

"Understood. See if you can find Kaiden in all this madness. I'm sure he could use your rifle."

"I need to sabotage any arrays they have in this area," the commander stated. "I'm sure they have the bulk of their forces in the main building, but they wouldn't connect each droid here to one terminal. That would be too easy for us. I'll go around and disable any other—"

"The droids are pouring out of the fort!" Wolfson bellowed on the open comms. "Hundreds are streaming into the main plaza."

Sasha muttered a curse under his breath. "I'm going. Take care of the other cannons as quickly as you can, Julio. Desmond, can we have air support for the ground troops?"

"I'm already working on it!" the Skyway Kings leader shouted. "I had to pull my jockeys back. Those droids are too accurate when in full force. The fighters will try to cut a path or at least deter them."

The commander pressed an escape switch and his pilot's chair leaned forward and dropped him down a hatch to the ground below. As he fell, he had a view of the robotic horde. Wolfson hadn't exaggerated as a stream of droids poured from the mouth of the main stronghold. Dozens in the front of the onslaught were already firing as several fighters swooped in above to deliver fusillades of missiles to annihilate two large groups at once. Many others simply pushed forward to replace the old and two of the fighters were disabled by a barrage of charged bolts. One impacted into a wall, while the other spun and crashed into a section of the army. At least he took some with him, although that was little comfort.

Sasha landed as another group of fighters streaked in to attack, but they had to break away when the droids turned their focus quickly on them. While it would buy the ground forces time to find cover, the fighters now had to weave and spin and dodge the blasts. They were only able to fire a few random shots from their main guns and a few missiles struck the perimeter of the enemy force with little damage.

"Zena, Janis, where are the reinforcements?" he demanded.

"I'm in the Zeppelin with the bulk of the droids," Janis responded. "But I sent two carriers' worth with Zena for faster transport."

"We'll be there in a few minutes, sir," she assured him. "I can see the gates."

He swore as another fighter spiraled out of the sky and landed only a couple of hundred yards away from him. "Isaac, scan for arrays, nodes, or anything that allows remote function," he ordered.

"I will compile a list as fast as I can, sir," the EI responded.

Sasha raised his sniper rifle and fired at the group through the gaps between buildings and warehouses. It was certainly not the most difficult feat he had ever accomplished, given the hundreds of droids on the march. Honestly, it would have been more impressive not to hit something.

He felled four droids in quick succession but several finally turned toward him. His eyes widened when their cannons snapped in his direction and began to charge. He grunted and sprinted out of range. These new models responded surprisingly quickly. The ground trembled with the residual force of an explosion behind him and he realized he would have to stay on the move. Hopefully, the other members of their team would realize the same thing.

Two more men fell when a round of lasers sank into their backs. That was seven so far that Kaiden had seen die. He howled in outrage as he hurled another thermal at the advancing droids. One simply caught it and flung it away. These bots were adapting. He'd thought they were merely better armored and geared, but they seemed to learn faster than any other metalhead he had fought in his life. Either that or whoever was controlling them was way more skilled than he gave them credit for.

He fired a blast at their feet, which thrust them back and provided enough time for him and the men behind him to get around the corner. Now that the droids had reached them, his team had actually moved back from where they had dropped and had to weave through the grid-like pattern of the buildings for cover and distance. One of the men stopped and charged his cannon and he followed suit to prepare a shot while two others readied their machine guns. When the bots appeared, they all fired as one to eliminate their pursuers before they could respond.

"Look up!" another shouted. The ace did so and scowled. Three droids perched on the ledge of one of the buildings, prepared to fire, but they were stopped when several small explosions detonated around them. Two fell over the side and two jet-jockeys flew overhead with a cheerful wave.

The ace tried to return the gesture but they spun hastily in an effort to dodge a sniper shot. One was hit in their pack, which ruptured and exploded and knocked the other one out of the sky. He grimaced and told the others to keep moving while he went to go check on the jockey. A machine gunner followed and he recognized the man's helmet as the one belonging to the gang member with the rosary.

They reached the fallen man, who struggled under a droid's leg that threatened to crush his chest. Kaiden raised his weapon but the machine gunner fired first. The strike flung the mechanical off the fallen merc but he hadn't vented his gun so it overheated. Their enemy simply focused on him and fired. The ace grabbed him and pulled him down and the lasers careened overhead. He fired and demolished the droid's legs. The body tumbled but it pushed itself up and aimed at them once more. He dropped Sire and drew Debonair to deliver three quick shots into its head and complete the job.

The machine gunner stood and proffered a hand. "Thanks," he said as he took it and the merc hauled him to his feet.

"Same to you," the gunner responded. "My name's Vick."

"I guess we didn't really have introductions on the ship," he recalled and shook quickly before releasing his hand. "I'm Kaiden."

"The gate isn't opening!" Fritz announced over the

comms in an irate voice. "They must have flushed the code out already."

"We're all dead if we can't get backup," the merc stated flatly.

Kaiden nodded. "It would take too long to blow through it, even if it's possible with what we have." He looked at Chief in his HUD. "We need to get it open. Where to, Chief?"

"Outside the main building. I pick up a terminal near the gate itself, probably a fallback method. Get me to it and I'll get it open," the EI promised.

He motioned for Vick to follow. "All ground troops, head to the main gate," he hollered into the comms. "We're gonna crack that thing open and need cover while we work." He received several responses. Some confirmed while others stated they were pinned down. Quite obviously, the gate was the priority now and they needed to move quickly.

The two moved through the winding paths and used the grid to their advantage as they darted around corners when they were set upon by droids. Opening the gate was their main focus, although after their last attack, he made sure to keep an eye on the roofs as well. The duo made a right turn and a trail of lasers from above shrieked down the line they had previously run through. A fighter banked and circled away. While he was thankful for the intervention, he also wished he had actually waited until they were out of the way rather than their safety simply being a happy coincidence. Things were becoming hectic.

When they were close to the gate, Chief nodded to him and disappeared to access the terminal. Two other groups

—one of heavies and the other mostly ground troops with shotguns and machine guns—joined forces. They brought company as several bots tailed each group. The two teams circled and fired with abandon through each line. While the maneuver funneled the droids directly to them, it was a mixed blessing as their numbers grew rapidly. It felt more like they were merely staving them off rather than actually decreasing their numbers. A group of jockeys landed on the roofs around them and fired at the unsuspecting droids to some effect. Unfortunately, it didn't take them long to react. Several switched their guns or cannons for arm blades and bounded up the buildings to drive the jockeys back. While some fought them off or took to the air, pained cries on the comms weren't encouraging.

Several large blasts from above pounded the mechanicals with impressive results. Kaiden grinned as Wolfson's ship circled. A few on the roof turned their attention to him as well. The ace charged a shot as they tried to aim at the ship, fired in the second it was ready, and swept them off the roof as the head officer pulled away to focus on another cannon.

"Got it!" Chief declared.

Several loud clicks confirmed that the main gate had unlocked and the doors began to pull apart. *"Keep it up. I'll stay in here in case they try to shut it again before everyone is inside."*

"To the main path," Kaiden ordered. They could meet the reinforcements as they poured in. The heavies cleared a route and one raised an arm to signal the others to follow. The group rushed out, firing behind them and above as they raced to the center. They fortunately didn't have to wait long. Once the first crack of light gleamed from the other side of the gate, it was immediately blocked by fighters in red, blue, or copper armor who surged inside. The new arrivals fired wildly as the doors opened wider and more raced into the fray. The droids finally began to retreat and find cover of their own when a couple of hundred troops joined the attack. More importantly, a large horde of their own mechanicals began to assault the enemy bots. Some even dropped in from above, having tried to climb the walls before the gate was opened and now finally made their way across.

A large whir sounded above and a giant ship appeared with pods all along the underside. These detached from the ship and descended in free-fall. The sides opened as soon as they landed and Azure Halo droids emerged, some even virtually on top of their opponents. Metal fists immediately engaged in a battle and hammered noisily into metal heads and chests.

The ace smiled as he vented his rifle. If those assholes in the tower thought they were trouble before, they were gonna cause some real chaos now.

CHAPTER TWENTY-SIX

"All troops, get out there and support the droids!" Lycan bellowed as the AO soldiers ran past him to join the fight. "Raz, I'll leave a contingent with you, but we need the cannons— Three are down? Well, that leaves three more. Use those. Then get them working!" he shouted as he dragged his battle gauntlets on and stormed down the hall.

Magellan peered around the corner and watched the feral man march away. He looked back and nodded. "It's probably best we don't try to confront him here directly."

"I won't argue with that," one of the hackers in the group muttered.

"We'll split up here, correct?" Cyra asked and readied her pistol.

"It seems the best place." The bounty hunter nodded and glanced at Chiyo. "Everyone knows where to go, right?"

"Of course. I'll handle the interior security while Cyra targets the robotics facility. When we have control, we can allow access for Kit's group to go in and take care of the core as well as let the soldiers inside to continue the fight."

He held up an explosive. "I'll cause a few distractions of my own. Are you sure you don't need me for backup?"

They both shook their head. "We're infiltrators. This is what we do."

"Fair enough." He chuckled and stowed the explosive. "But be careful. I'm sure most of the trouble is outside, but you're still likely to run into a couple of droids and security along the way, and I'm sure that whoever is running the places you want to take over won't simply lie down for you."

"We'll be convincing," Chiyo stated. "We need to hurry."

Magellan jogged down the center hall. The two women nodded to each other before the group separated into two teams, one with six members and the other with five.

Cyra and her five teammates were the first to run into opposition—two turrets hanging on the ceiling above the next hallway. She held her arm up and a holoconsole appeared around her gauntlet. These should be easy enough to control, if only temporarily. Metallic footsteps alerted her to a group of ten droids that turned into the corridor and she smiled when she realized this would work out well.

She connected to the turrets' systems, issued the override command, and watched the link-up percentage gain as the mechanicals marched closer. Behind her, the other members of her team armed themselves quietly. A checkmark appeared when the command completed. It had taken eight seconds, which was longer than normal.

The turrets turned as the droids passed under them, fired, and destroyed about four before the others turned to retaliate. The infiltrator released the connection and transferred her focus to taking control of the remaining enemy. She managed to commandeer two a second before the turrets fell. The connection time had taken eleven seconds, and the control wasn't strong. She wished she had more time to study what was some powerful security for remote OS.

Unfortunately, she had other priorities. She directed the mechanicals she had control of to turn and fire on the others, keeping their backs to her as she ran out. Two others remained and she drew her pistol and charged it while she grasped the back of one of the defender's head. Electricity arced out of her glove and fried it as the other turned and an arm blade unsheathed. She simply raised her pistol and fired at its face at point-blank range.

Her adversary teetered noisily but didn't go down, and she stumbled back but righted herself quickly and prepared to attack again. Several other shots resounded from behind her and saved her the effort. She grinned and looked at her team with a wave of thanks for their assistance before they pressed on.

Chiyo opened a door cautiously, hoping to get out of sight of approaching droids. She froze and aimed instinctively when she saw more mechanicals within. These, however, were immobile and no power seemed to emanate from them at all. Kaitō would have let her know if something was amiss. The group filed inside quickly and waited for the patrol to pass while she studied the inactive robots.

"Do you think they are defective?" she asked one of the hackers after a moment.

He shrugged and moved to the back of one to take a look. "They look like older models and don't have some of the same details in the rig as I've seen on the others."

"Do you think we should take them?" another asked.

"That's exactly what I think." She estimated that there were about eight in there that she could see and more could be stored in the pods in the back. It was more likely, though, that they'd been disassembled for parts or in preparation for reworks.

"Can we get them running?" she asked.

"They're missing power units, but those should be easy enough to find," the first hacker stated and motioned for another to come over. "Sala, do you have any spare drives with a droid OS? These are probably smoked."

"I have one," she said and held up a small rectangular drive. "I can copy it to others if we have spares."

"Give it here," he stated and held his hand out. "I'll install it in this one and have it connect to the others and daisy-chain it. That'll be easier and faster."

"Good call." Chiyo nodded and raised her pistol. "We're close to the security room. I'll have a look around and when those are ready, we'll take it by force."

"Got it." He nodded. She opened the door and peered out in both directions to confirm that neither droids nor guards were present. Cautiously, she darted out and a hasty scan of the area identified a vent that would have access into the security room. She retrieved a multi-tool and opened the grate, clambered in, and followed the tunnel.

When she finally made her way to their destination, at least a dozen people worked on several consoles and clearly tried to reactivate or purge the systems Fritz had tampered with.

"Cannons are almost ready!" one shouted to a man in the middle of the room who worked on several holo-screens at once.

"When they are activated, blow as many of them away as you can," he instructed. "I'll have the droids hunt those who try to get away."

Chiyo couldn't let them get the cannons online. Even a few blasts could cause the attack to falter. Her expression grim, she focused on the console and activated her tech suite.

Raz stiffened and frowned when he had an odd reading from one of the consoles. The screen flashed and the tech-nician working on the machine scrambled quickly to try to fix whatever had gone wrong, but he had seen this before.

"Interesting. A little techie spy is among us," he whis-pered and a smile formed on his lips. "Finally, I have someone intriguing to work with."

***

Chiyo drifted between several cubes. The optimum attack would be to restructure them to suit her needs, but she didn't have the time to locate each correct node and simply resorted to destroying or powering down as many as she found. She froze when everything shimmered around her. The blue, iridescent sky-like area above turned dark and red, while the nodes changed to various black shapes that made it difficult to distinguish between them. All the streams of data she had grown accustomed to had become mist-like and whirled in a frenzy rather than flowed as a steady wave.

"And who might you be?" She spun to locate the source of the voice and recognized the man who had stood in the center of the room. He held his hands behind his back and hovered only a few yards away from her, dressed in pants and a shirt that seemed too long and wide for his thin frame. Although she could see micro-chain in the lining, he didn't wear typical armor and instead, simply had a guard around his mouth and a visor over his eyes.

The infiltrator glanced furtively around while she tried to assess the situation. She had bought a little time but this man had obviously done something since and she didn't know if he had already righted what she had wronged.

"So you're not going to answer?" Raz asked and held a hand up. "Fine. I had hoped for even a little real conversation after having to deal with the boring babble of these other techies, but if you don't want to oblige, I'll simply have to be rid of you that much quicker."

Several of the nodes transformed into drones that immediately began to fire at her. She backed away quickly and tried to find safety behind others, but the same process repeated no matter where she went. In desperation, she paused at a pool of the data mist and tried to see if she could replicate whatever it was he was doing, but to no avail.

"You're not used to someone having this kind of complete control, are you?" he asked teasingly as his creations continued their pursuit. His voice carried to her no matter how far away she was. "My EI, although I'm sure it's not to the level of yours, has my personal touch," he explained and grinned when several shots struck her. She spiraled down but managed to right herself and continued to flee—probably, he reasoned, in an attempt to find a point far enough away that she could safely disengage from. Even if she did, it was no matter. Even a small time in his domain would wrack the mind. It should be a simple matter to find and finish her.

In the next moment, she disappeared. But while her body was visibly absent, Raz still felt an odd sensation that implied another presence in his space. Was there another infiltrator he hadn't seen? Suddenly, his brain pulsed and pain throbbed through him as he tried quickly to force himself out of the suite. Despite his desperate effort, something prevented him from disengaging.

"A basic rule of spycraft is to keep your ideas or talents a secret," a female voice stated in his head. "I was blindsided by your attack, but if this is merely the work of a cracker EI, that's much easier to disassemble—although I don't know about the repercussions to you, given that you're using it right now."

"W-w-wait!" he cried, but the world around him began to crack and disintegrate in front of him. He slid through darkness with no point of return or floor to fall to.

Raz's body stumbled back and collapsed, alarming some of the other techs as his screens went blank.

Chiyo, sweating and breathing deep to adjust after the infiltrator suite deactivated, took a moment to rest and rub her temples.

"They're ready, Chiyo," the Halo hacker informed her.

"Good, they're distracted." She shuffled in the vent to turn and head to the exit. "Let's deal with them quickly and take control."

CHAPTER TWENTY-SEVEN

Sasha ripped off the terminal covering, placed his pistol against the exposed plate, and fired several shots into the array. He stepped back when it began to spark and smoke. A small fire began as the lights died and the energy readings faded.

"One left, sir," Isaac informed him. *"Should you keep this up, your completion time for this objective will be among your best."*

"It only matters if it's effective, Isaac," he reminded his EI.

He began to move out when a loud voice demanded over the comms, "Sasha, are you there?"

"Julio?" he responded and after a hasty scrutiny to confirm that his position was secure, he leaned behind the relative protection of the walls. "Is everything proceeding well? The cannons haven't come back on, have they?"

"No, Wolfson and I have destroyed most of them, and I assume the hackers are in position by now," Julio reasoned.

"But another wave is coming out—more droids, but there are guards on the field now as well."

The commander pushed off the wall, turned, and vaulted up to grab the edge of the roof. He hauled himself up carefully and positioned his rifle to look through the scope at the entrance of the main building. Dozens of soldiers raced out decked out in white and gold armor and wielding obviously modified weapons. "It's less of a complication and more of an annoyance," he muttered and lowered his weapon. "Have the fighters make another assault, but be wary of mounted cannons and turrets along the roofs or on the—"

"Sir, incoming projectile—dive back!" Isaac warned as his HUD flashed red. Sasha obeyed and rolled off the building. A bullet clipped the edge of the roof a second after he landed.

"What was that, Isaac? A gyro round?" he asked as he moved into a jog.

"Indeed, sir, from a new opponent. None of the robotic hostiles have been tracked as using that kind of ammunition."

Sasha nodded. "Another marksman. A pity Magellan isn't around to deal with them." He lowered the output of his rifle's core and inserted a magazine of kinetic rounds into the weapon. "I won't be able to go about my business as I please if I'm in their sights. I guess I won't add a new accomplishment to my objective time."

"Perhaps you could, sir," Isaac said encouragingly. *"We'll see how long it takes you to eliminate this assailant."*

Lycan marched out of the building and sneered at a trio of fighter ships that rocketed down from above. He drew his cannon from his waist holster and charged it while he aimed at the one in the middle. When he fired, the orb traveled much faster than any normal cannon blast and pounded into the underside of the ship. A brief flash of orange lines coursed through the vessel before it exploded. The blast caught the ship on the right and inflicted enough damage that it began to spiral and crashed into a nearby building. Despite being thrown off course by the force, the remaining ship was able to right itself and break away.

The large man huffed as he walked past a couple of soldiers who stared at him in shock. He gazed coolly at them as he charged another shot. "Man the cannons and eliminate their air support," he ordered as he fired at another ship to sheer its wings off. He grinned when it plummeted. "And mind your heads."

They nodded and ran off as his comm link activated. "What is it, Cascina?"

"I'm tracking a sniper and he's rather nimble, I have to say," she explained. He could hear a click over the comms as she reloaded. "But more importantly, I have the triangulate array online. It looks like we still have a more than two-to-one advantage."

"You got it online?" he questioned. "What about Raz? The tech stuff is why we keep him around!"

"He might still be busy with the tampering," she suggested. "The main cannons are still down—the two remaining, anyway."

He clenched his teeth and stared out over the battle. As much as he wanted to literally jump into the fray, if any of them would fuck this up, it would be Raz. "I'll head back in and take a look," he stated and spun to return to the building. "Jalloh can keep an eye on the troops."

"He's already inside," Cascina told him. "He never left."

Lycan scowled. "Why?"

Magellan placed the last of his explosives against an important-looking machine. He had to admit he was essentially playing by ear right now and most of this equipment wasn't something he was familiar with. But these were powerful explosives. He was sure he would damage something of value.

He left the room, checked the hall, and drew his rifle to shorten the barrel. "Ladies, I wanted to let you know I've primed the explosives," he announced over the link. "Are you both in position?"

"If our map is correct, I should be in the robotics facility in only a couple of minutes," Cyra replied.

"We've taken the security center," Chiyo stated, breathing heavily. "We'll be set up soon."

"Are you all right, Chiyo?" he inquired when he noted her labored speech.

"I'll be fine," she promised. "But I'm glad I spent more time getting used to the suite."

Cyra laughed over the comms. "Time well spent, eh?" Her jovial tone changed quickly to one of concern. "Uh… Chi, do you mind making a quick change to focus on clearing my path?"

"I can. What's wrong?" She gasped. "The connections have changed. They aren't on the main systems anymore."

"What does that mean?" the bounty hunter asked as he picked up his pace.

"It means she can't shut anything in this sector down," Cyra replied. Laser fire crackled over her comm. "I can't get control of the defenses over here, and more droids are heading our way. Someone was waiting for us."

"I'm on my way!" He grasped his rifle in both hands and sprinted down the hall until he found an elevator, blasted the doors off, and leapt down the shaft.

Kaiden yanked his plasma blade out of the Arbiter droid's head and slid it into its container before he twisted and raised his rifle when he heard numerous footsteps behind him. He released a relieved sigh when he saw the black and dark-blue colors of the Halos and Kit leading the group.

"It's good to see you made it in all right," he said and nodded to her. "Are you heading to the main base?"

"Yeah. We're behind schedule already," she replied and continued to run as he kept pace. "My guess is the others are already in position but no matter how good they are, someone will realize something is wrong eventually. I'd rather have the place locked down and ready to blow before they decide to turn that army around."

"I won't argue." He caught the attention of a few Riders and Kings along the way and indicated for them join the group. "We'll help you make up for the lost time. It might not be the most covert approach, but considering we have the cover of—" A large explosion detonated on the roof of a building several yards away and two jockeys jetted away in its wake. "Yeah, the cover of all of that, I think we can afford to be loud."

"It's a mixed bag," she responded as they ran to the far wall to try to inch around the center of the fighting. "It might act as a cover, but the two potential entries we hoped to use are both surrounded by hostiles. It basically means a death march if we try to use them now, so do you have any other suggestions?"

He gave it some thought and sighed. "I guess it all depends on what we see when we get closer, but I have to ask, how do you feel about vents?"

"I'm claustrophobic," she replied. He couldn't tell if she was serious or not. "Do you have any other suggestions?"

The ace lowered a hand to his belt. "I have a few thermals left. If you have something that can juice them up, maybe we can blow a hole in the wall?"

She retrieved some kind of pronged device from her own belt and nodded. "We'll go with that."

CHAPTER TWENTY-EIGHT

Dario sat on the edge of Tory Harper's bed and waited with growing impatience while her body disintegrated with faint pops of amber light. The female golem sat in a chair across from him. Blond hair began to emerge from its skull. Its eye shape contorted and the color changed from a pale white to the council member's sapphire blue.

He yawned, more out of boredom than weariness. This would make three so far and it should hopefully take less than a day for him to complete the fourth and final transformation. One would think people with this degree of political clout would have better security. It really would have been far more interesting if they had. Well, it was probably time for him to check-in, which would no doubt bring a measure of satisfaction. He wanted to surprise Merrick with his swiftness but he also had time to burn.

When he turned his connection on, he saw a number of messages appear in his HUD. One from Nolan, a few from Jalloh, and finally, Merrick. When he opened his boss' message, all he received was a video feed which revealed that their Fenris facility was currently in the middle of a siege.

Apparently, the world had caught fire in the last few hours. He sent a message to Merrick. *What do you need?*

Get going, was the instant reply. He stood and the cigar was immediately enveloped in nanos that dispersed in seconds. The golem would complete its transformation successfully without him so there really was no reason to not leave and board his ship.

Cyra tried to aid the limping hacker but he was dead before she could reach him. Instead, she was grabbed from the back and hauled behind the defensive barrier.

Several of her team fired at the advancing droids, while the others tried to take control of the turrets, emergency doors, or anything else that might swing the tide in their favor. Their efforts proved fruitless.

"Are we locked out?" she asked and looked around for any possible means of escape. Thus far. they'd merely been stopped from advancing, but if they activated the defenses behind them, they would be trapped. She had to make a decision soon.

"More or less," one of the hacker's confirmed, his voice tight with frustration. "It's more like we can't get hold of anything in the first place. Every time we are close to gaining entry—or hell, simply try to shut them down—the system switches to a new array."

Whoever had taken control of the defenses in this

sector constantly bounced the control signals of the defenses to several different arrays, a rudimentary but very effective defense against hackers, at least in a small space. She could probably gather the info for the different arrays and find a workaround, but while the team was currently getting mowed down, she didn't exactly have the time.

Several shots whined overhead but from their side, this time. They hammered into a few of the droids and felled them while another two destroyed the blaster turret that peppered their barrier. Magellan advanced, reached behind him for a cylinder attached to his pack, and threw it to her. She caught it and understood what he wanted to do as soon as she recognized it. He helped the other hackers keep the attackers at bay while she worked on the emitter to alter the output vector and energy conversion.

"It's ready!" she yelled. The bounty hunter hustled the group behind the barrier to a safer position around the corner as Cyra activated the device and raced to join them. The emitter glowed brightly before it suddenly went dark, along with all the lights, barrier, and remaining droids that simply froze, lost power, and collapsed.

One of the hackers looked around the corner, his head tilted in bemusement. "An EMP?"

"Technically, it's an emission device to power my weapons and armor," Magellan explained. He removed a small box and placed it into a slot on his rifle before he powered it on again. "I worked with a hacker before who jerry-rigged it into an EMP device in the past. I kind of hedged my bets that you knew how to do the same thing."

"Fortunately, that was a basic lesson back in my days at the Academy but it's been a while since I had to dust it off."

Cyra chuckled as she retrieved a shielded charge with several lines, drew one line out, and connected it to her gauntlet. She offered the others to the group. "Restart your systems. We have to move. I'm sure whoever sent those bots after us is doing the same in the facility."

A few of the hackers took the extra lines and connected them to their charging ports. Others had their own devices to quickly restart their armor and gear. Magellan removed the box from his rifle once it had reactivated and placed it on his helmet. "I'll go ahead and take care of the sneaky little bastard who's waiting for us."

She nodded. "Be careful. I'm sure they have backup, and the EMP was only a temporary fix. The droids and defenses will be back online soon."

"Understood." He nodded and began to walk away before he called over his shoulder. "If you could recover and join me sooner rather than later, it would be much appreciated."

"We'll be right behind you," she promised. "We still have a job to do."

Kaiden, Kit, and her team all stood well back as a massive explosion powered through the right side of the ground floor of the stronghold central building. When the smoke cleared, a few droids stepped out of the new entrance and paused to scan for a disturbance.

"Good Lord. They never end," he muttered as the invaders raised their weapons but a hail of laser fire swept into the droids. They held up much longer than he would have thought, although the constant barrage didn't give them the time to react. The mechanicals withstood the assault for a few seconds before they succumbed, and Kit raised a hand to stop the attack and move forward.

The group ventured inside as another loud explosion erupted in the battle.

"Shit!" the head officer shouted over the comms.

"Wolfson?" Kaiden called frantically. "Are you okay?"

"I'm fine but I had to bail from my ship." He sounded furious.

"Do you need back up?" the ace asked as Kit and a few of the hackers looked back.

"I'll be fine, boyo." The assurance was followed by a large clang, probably from Wolfson drawing his shotgun. "I wanted to get my boots on the ground anyway. They might have taken my ship but that doesn't mean my count will drop."

"All right." He nodded. "I'm with Kit. We're inside the building. Let me know if you need any backup."

"You're in? Good, but be wary. I saw some big bastard shoot down a couple of ships earlier on. Before I could return the favor, he stormed inside, so be on the lookout for him along with anything else."

Wolfson—the giant—described the man as a big bastard? If he thought he was big, God help a normal person who encountered him. If he was already inside, he was either trying to round up more soldiers or... He looked at the Rider and King troops. "You stay with her. I have to go."

"What's wrong?" she asked, concerned.

"I think you were right. They have already learned

about the other teams," he stated as he broke into a jog and tried to contact Chiyo. "And they are taking action."

"The prisoners are secure!" one of the hackers called as he checked the group of six techies who had surrendered and were currently being guarded by a trio of hacked repurposed droids that aimed cannons at them.

"Good. Now we can focus on taking control of what we can," Chiyo stated and focused on the darkened area of the map. "We'll need Cyra to get that sector of the building back onto the main system, though."

A loud thud on the door startled them all. Two of the droids approached and readied their weapons as the pounding continued. She tried to check the cameras, but they were all blown out or disabled, ironically by their own actions. The noise ceased but two more droids approached, along with some of the hackers with their weapons drawn. It was frighteningly quiet now, but as she drew her own weapon and walked closer, she could hear a distinctive beeping.

"Get back!" she yelled a split-second before an explosion ripped the doors off. They careened into one of the droids and flattened it against a wall. Two orbs hurtled in through the smoke, detonated, and destroyed several of the robots. Two of the hackers were also caught in the blast and they shrieked in pain as their armor melted against their skin.

One of the prisoners tried to flee and was instantly felled by the guards, but the others used the chaos to escape as the droids flipped their aim constantly from them to the new threat. One of the Halos ordered the mechanicals to stop them, but when they fired after the retreating prisoners, their attacks were blocked by a large red shield.

A large man walked through the entry holding the projected barrier and snarled when he looked around the room. He sneered at Raz's unconscious body. "Dammit, you had the easy job," he muttered as he refocused on the room and brandished a cannon—one a normal person would have to hold in two hands, but he wielded like it was a personal hand cannon.

Chiyo activated the defensive turrets. They dropped from above and aimed at the intruder, but he simply raised his weapon as their shots were absorbed by his shield. He fired and caught a couple of the turrets but the impact of the attack destroyed the ceiling. The remaining Halos scrambled to avoid the lethal metal pieces that plummeted as the overhead structure caved in.

She fell back as metal bounced off her armor. The ground rumbled and she glanced at the giant. He stared curiously at her but also seemed more than a little angry.

"That wasn't a smart move, techie."

CHAPTER TWENTY-NINE

Magellan was able to crack the door to the facility open. He placed both hands on the left door and shoved hard and was able to force one side apart enough for him to enter. The enhanced vision of his visor guided him as he walked into the bowels of the facility. Ahead of him, large racks appeared to be assembly lines for parts and armor. He inspected them quickly. Most pieces were in various states of assembly, but what unnerved him was that when he looked farther down the lines, he found massive racks with numerous droid units ready for final construction.

What they were fighting out there seemed to be only a third of what was possible if they had attacked even only a few days later. It reminded him of how often luck and foresight could play into winning a battle.

A few metallic items clinked along the floor behind him. He flinched but didn't immediately turn. His opponent wouldn't be so careless and probably tried deliberately to draw his attention. He powered his rifle down and holstered it before he turned a dial on the side of his helmet to increase the audio input into his headset. In the silence, he listened calmly for the hum of a gun's core, ragged breathing, or even a misplaced step. His opponent would most likely be above him, using the railings and tall machinery to easily traverse the room. He hadn't seen any traps, so he was likely waiting for the internal defenses to reset to regain his advantage.

The bounty hunter eased his hand to his gauntlet in preparation. A click behind him and up to the left identified his adversary. He stood between the racks and a quick hum confirmed that he primed his weapon. Magellan whirled as the gun fired, raised his arm, and pressed the button he had held his hand on. A reflector activated and boomeranged the shot. The attacker was fast but it still clipped him enough that he lost his balance and he fell from the racks. As the enemy twisted to land on his feet, the bounty hunter drew his pistol, held the trigger down, and fired several shots while he used his free hand to lower the volume on his helmet.

A couple of the shots struck home but didn't do much good. The assailant had apparently been able to get his gear working as well and his shielding absorbed the shots. He retaliated without hesitation and either switched weapons or activated full-auto to deliver a fusillade of lasers at his target.

Magellan flipped over one of the assembly lines and hunkered into the cover it provided. He holstered his pistol and drew his rifle, rolled behind one of the machines, and found a position at an angle to his opponent's aim. If the man wanted a clean shot, he would have to vault over the assembly line as well to reach him, and he would easily bet on himself being the quicker shot.

Instead, the room fell silent again and it seemed the attacker had once again gone on the prowl. The bounty hunter glanced at the door and wondered if he would try to sneak out and target Cyra and her team while they were still reorganizing. More dinging noises clinked from several different directions. Obviously, the sniper now tried to distract him. With an inward sigh, he reached for his audio switch again but hesitated. If his opponent was aware of that trick, he could simply set off a small explosion or drop a few of the hanging droid rigs to deafen him while he listened using the enhanced audio.

Something clicked, followed by a high-pitched screech that told him something was coming online. Magellan acted on instinct and raised his rifle quickly. A droid aimed at him from where it hung on the racks above. He fired and caught it squarely in its unarmored chest. Something fell as the mechanical powered down and he recognized that it was a gun. The sniper had used his gun's core to briefly power the droid. *Shit!*

He pivoted and held his rifle up as his attacker plunged toward him with a plasma blade in hand. A vicious swipe seared the blade into the side of the rifle barrel. The bounty hunter had paid good credits to make sure the barrel was reinforced in case he had to defend himself at close quarters, but the heat of the blade still gouged into it as they struggled against one another. He grimaced when his assailant drew his other arm back and a long blade jutted from the top of it. With a swift, unexpected twist, he kneed his attacker in the chest and flipped his rifle to thump him in the side of his helmet with the butt.

His adversary collided with the side of the assembly line. Magellan dropped the rifle, drew his pistol once again, and prepared to fire when the man thrust his arm forward and the long blade fired out of the gauntlet. He tilted his head instinctively but it still slid along the side of his neck. A hiss escaped him as he fought the shock of the deep incision and the man turned and flipped his plasma blade to go for the kill. The bounty hunter had little room to maneuver but was determined not to fall back. In fact, he let the blade strike him in the chest where his armor was thickest and caught his opponent by the arm in a surprise attack. He raised a leg, drove it into the man's knee, and held him as he fell, then placed the barrel of his gun against his foe's helmet.

The man looked up and his visor slid to the side, a small admission of defeat. "Can I have your name?"

The bounty hunter nodded before he pulled the trigger. "Magellan Desperaux."

He closed his eyes. "Well fought."

Lycan hurled the hacker who clung to his arm into the wall and glowered at Chiyo, who fiddled with the device on her arm.

"Are you trying to hack my gear?" he asked with a smirk. "It's no good. You techie types are easy pickings for me. I don't have anything fancy for you to try to get your slimy little—" His words broke off when a redline appeared on the left of his screen. For once, he was shocked. "Jalloh?" he whispered as the vital sign vanished.

He dragged in a deep breath and trembled a little before he uttered a furious howl. "You goddamned bastards!" he roared as he drew his cannon and began to fire randomly in a blind rage. The infiltrator and her remaining team either dove for cover or tried to get out of the room. He was forced to stop firing when the weapon overheated and he began to swing it wildly to shatter the consoles and other equipment. He kicked and stamped on both the already destroyed droids and unconscious bodies alike.

Chiyo, however, used the chaos to finish what she had started. She had already deduced that all his equipment couldn't be sabotaged, although she wished she had come up with whatever had set him off. Instead, she completed her mission to shut down the interior defenses in case this beast of a man destroyed the place—which seemed very likely. But as she finished and all sections of the building she had access to went dark, Lycan caught her with a backhand and flipped her. She landed awkwardly and banged the back of her helmet against the hard floor. As she tried to force herself to her feet, he snatched her by the neck, lifted her up, and pressed the heated barrel of his cannon into her abdomen.

He snarled at her while the heat of the barrel began to burn through her underlay and dug it deeper as if he tried to skewer her with it.

"Purge!" she cried and the power in her shields expunged to create a wave of energy, enough to thrust him back and loosen his grip. She kicked off his chest to finally wrench herself free. He had already recovered when she landed and lunged at her with his cannon raised. She stared helplessly, all out of options, but an orb of green energy rocketed into his chest and shoved him back a few feet before it exploded and drove him into the wall, which cratered with the force of impact.

Kaiden walked up, already charging another shot. "Are you done here?" he asked.

She nodded and gestured for any of the hackers who could still walk to help move the unconscious or wounded out of the room. "I have access to most of the systems and I've shut down what I can."

"Good. Kit is getting into position and we'll wrap this up soon. Where's Cyra?"

Before she could answer, Lycan charged out of the hole in the wall. The ace fired another shot but his gauntlet glowed red and he simply released the orb as they flung themselves to the side to dodge the giant.

Kaiden vented his rifle as Chiyo drew her sub-machine gun. "What did you do to piss him off?" he asked.

"I think something happened to a teammate of his," she explained and aimed as their adversary turned and finally vented his cannon. "But you did shoot him into the wall."

"Fair enough," he admitted as he closed Sire's vent. "I'll go for the head this time."

CHAPTER THIRTY

W olfson shoved the barrel of his shotgun into the chest of a droid and fired with a broad grin. He continued to run down the line and fired at any droid in his path while four Rider heavies provided backup with chain gun fire that obliterated the mechanicals in wide swaths to either side.

"This is hardly better than dummy practice," the security officer hollered. He retrieved a metal stick, pressed a button on the side that revealed a plasma blade in the shape of a hatchet, and cleaved into the side of a droid's head. "They've gone sluggish. Is this your doing, Sasha?"

"Perhaps, in a minimal way," the commander conceded and his breathing seemed to have grown slightly heavier. "I've yet to destroy the last array, so I would think that this is due to Cyra and her team's efforts, but I can't establish a link with them."

He lodged the plasma ax into another droid's chest and fired his shotgun at one that tried to approach behind him. Something clunked into the side of his head and his visor cracked as he toppled. He felt his helmet gingerly and found a hole through which he could feel the foam touching his scalp and grunted as he unlocked his headgear and yanked it off.

"Sasha! You haven't dealt with that sniper."

"I've been a little distracted," the other man retorted and a shot echoed in the comms. "On top of that, she's using a stealth generator. Isaac can't locate her unless I'm close."

"How close?" Wolfson asked and glanced in the direction of the shot.

"About twenty to twenty-five meters," the marksman explained.

He flipped the ax decisively. "I'll get 'em to come out. You be ready to take 'em out," he ordered as he barreled forward to find the sniper. He hacked and blasted his way through the horde as several jockeys landed around him, followed by a couple of dozen of their droids that immediately entered the fray. They were finally pushing back.

Lycan shut the vent on his cannon and took a moment to look at his chest. Although he still growled with real annoyance, he did have the look of someone mildly impressed. "You're a sneaky little bastard," he muttered and glared at Kaiden. "But that was a good strike."

"I didn't exactly tip-toe around," he retorted. "I sprinted down the hall, in fact. You're merely a big-ass target." He tilted his head to the side and studied him. "You also seem familiar."

"He was part of that team at the arena on Vox," Chiyo explained. "I thought the same thing when I first saw him."

"You're the one who beat Jaxon," he stated angrily as the memory became clear.

The man's face contorted between his anger and newfound amusement. "The last time we were at Arena-Max... Yeah, that Tsuna." He shook his head. "I told Jalloh we should have simply dealt with you there. We were supposed to eliminate some Nexus students and a group happened to be on Vox? It was too much of a coincidence." His face finally set into a grim frown. "I guess I'll make up for the mistake."

"Kaiden, keep him in place," Chiyo whispered over the comm. "Look above."

He risked a furtive glance and noticed a string of cables and wires, nodded to her, and raised his rifle. "The mistake was working for the AO, and we'll correct that."

The giant snorted and held his gauntlet up, which began to glow red. "You have no idea who you're messing with, kid—neither me nor them." He attacked as Kaiden fired and Chiyo broke off to the side. The large man once again batted the charged shot aside, but the ace had only charged it halfway and quickly fired another while he was in mid-swing. This one struck him in the stomach, thrust him back, and cracked his armor. Kaiden holstered his rifle, retrieved his shield emitter, and activated it as he lunged into the larger man.

Damn, he was strong. His feet scrabbled for purchase as Lycan tried to force him back while his other hand moved to his cannon. "Dumbass, what are you trying to prove?" he asked and prepared to fire.

Chiyo leapt up, grasped his shoulder, and hoisted herself up. She snatched one of the cables above the giant and stabbed it into the back of his neck. He shrieked as a surge of electricity sizzled through him. His erratic jerks dislodged the infiltrator and she fell as her partner broke away and covered them both with his shield. Their adversary's gauntlets began to spark and in seconds, they burst to burn and mangle his hands. His cannon clattered free and his body soon followed to collapse face-first.

The ace deactivated the shield and helped Chiyo to her feet. "Do you think he's dead?"

"I pick up a faint pulse," Chief informed him. *"Do you wanna finish it?"*

He looked at the man's burnt, crippled hands. "I don't think he's in any shape to run off or fight back for now."

"And as a contracted member of the organization, he'll be useful for information, possibly even in testimony," she added.

Kaiden shrugged. "The first part, maybe, but I don't think we can get our hopes that high."

"Either way, I was able to get some data about this facility before he trashed most of the consoles," she continued. "But nothing more than some of their server information and security protocols. Nothing of much use outside of the facility."

"I ran past a ton of different server rooms and offices on the way here. One of them is bound to have something."

"I have a location," she stated and showed him a map on her tablet. "Part of those security protocols mentioned this room several times. I'm sure they are storing something of importance there."

"That's near Kit," he pointed. "I need to get back there and make sure everything is okay."

She nodded and put her tablet away. "Go on ahead. I need to check on the rest of my team and we'll head over if everyone is in good enough shape."

"Okay." He nodded and drew his rifle once more. "And good job with the giant. It seems you can cause as much of a ruckus as I can on occasion."

"About as much as you can remain quiet," she teased and headed out the door. "We're close, Kaiden. Let's finish this."

He nodded, about to say he agreed when a garbled voice spoke over the comms. "Ca...ne...hear me?"

"Who is this?" he asked and noticed that the infiltrator had also stopped to listen.

"Cy...a... Thi...is Cyra." The woman's voice cleared suddenly. "The power was knocked out. I'm trying to get everything back to normal, but comms are still in short range. Can you hear me?"

"Perfectly now," Chiyo stated. "Are you all right?"

"Me and my team are finally in the facility and shutting everything down," she explained. "We're fine now, thanks to Magellan, but he's hurt. He had some medical supplies we've used to help him out, but he needs evac."

"I'll get Julio to swing around," the ace said quickly. "He should still be in the air and has the space. If you have explosives, blow a hole in the wall and ping your position. If not, ping your position and make sure your heads are down. He'll take care of it."

"Speaking of explosives, Kaiden," Magellan added, his voice shallow and weak. "I have a few planted on the upper and middle levels. I planned to use them if they decided to return and take their base back. You could still use them if necessary."

"I'll keep that in mind," he stated. "But Kit is at their core now, and if we have to, we can blow this entire place to smithereens."

The bounty hunter chuckled. "I guess that means my little bombs are simply rather quaint now, eh?"

"You were a great help, Magellan," Cyra assured him.

"You hold tight, Magellan," Kaiden ordered. "I'll get on the line with Julio and let him know to swing around, Cyra."

"Understood," she answered. "Thank you."

They signed off and he glanced at Chiyo. "I guess we're closer to wrapping this up than we thought."

"The droids are still activated," Chief noted. *"I guess their main control wasn't in the facility."*

"Then I would assume it's in the main power station with Kit—or the room I'll be heading to," she reasoned.

"Then let's get this done," the ace demanded. "We've been here a little over an hour, now, and we've definitely sent a message to the organization, but I don't think we want to be here if they want to reply."

She nodded. "Agreed."

CHAPTER THIRTY-ONE

Wolfson kicked down the door to one of the storage units and a small lighting device activated on his shoulder plate to emit several thin green beams as he walked slowly inside. A jockey had notified him that he saw the sniper run into this section of the plaza after their stealth generator dropped. Either they were running low on energy or they were wounded.

A trap was also possible, or they could have fallen back here to— Wait, was that array Sasha was looking for over there? The lights continued to scan the room in a cone shape. Without his helmet, he hoped to catch his quarry by having the lights refract off their cloaking. At a thud to his left, he turned and fired his shotgun to demolish a barrel and pepper holes into a box of parts but there was no sniper or active droid. He was getting tunnel vision and needed to remain alert. The droids had become active again out there so they weren't out of the woods yet.

A crunch at the door made him whirl in that direction. He almost fired when he saw the bright eyes but he noted the blue colors in time. They were droids but those on their team. They entered the room, their blades at the ready on their arms, and he turned to continue his exploration but paused when something occurred to him. Why were they there? The droids were supposed to be on the front lines, not wandering about. *Shit.*

The security officer yanked his arm back to drive his ax in a blind blow behind him. It dug into one of the hacked droids' chest as it tried to sneak up on him. The arm still descended and he raised his shoulder defensively. The blade bounced off his armor but sliced his light emitter off. He booted the droid off his weapon as the other tried to leap on top of him. Wolfson caught it by the neck on the underside of his blade, hurled it down, and fired his shotgun into its head. His first assailant was apparently not quite as dead as he thought and raised an arm to fire the blade at him. He thwacked the weapon out of the air with his ax before he delivered two shots at the stubborn robot. One felled it and the other was simply for good measure. The lights in its eyes died as he walked up to it and triggered another lighting device from the opposite shoulder, this one a normal flashlight.

As he examined the mechanical, he caught something in his image as it reflected off the metal chest. A red line streaked from his chest to his head. *Shit!* Wolfson raised his ax in the same moment that a shot was fired. The blade exploded and shards speared into his face as he scrambled back and emptied his shotgun in the direction of the laser light. Most seemed to strike the railing, walls, or ceiling in his blind fire, but at least a couple found their mark.

A pained shout was quickly followed by the thump of

something hitting the floor. He tossed the handle of his blade aside and reloaded. The sniper's cloak fell away and he lost a second to surprise when he realized it was a woman. She drew her pistol and took aim at the security officer. He raised one arm and two kinetic rounds lodged into his gauntlet. With his free hand, he raised his weapon as a third bullet seared along the side of his forehead.

Wolfson fired and gripped his weapon tightly to right it from the kickback. His assailant had rolled away but some of the spread caught her side. Still, she staggered to her feet and vaulted over a conveyor belt. He fired again and heard only the loud clank of metal.

"Sasha, she's at my position!" he called. "She'll get away!"

"She won't," the commander stated calmly. A door at the other end of the building began to slide open in the same moment that the woman reactivated her cloak. "Sasha!"

A figure appeared in the doorway. The loud report of a rifle was followed by another thump. Sasha flipped his rifle and aimed it at the fallen sniper while Wolfson hurried over. The woman's cloak dissipated as quickly as it had activated.

"Humph." The large man grunted and slung his shotgun over his shoulder. "Were you simply waiting to make some grand entrance?"

"I was on the other side of the battlefield, Wolfson," the other man explained and moved past his friend. "I also assumed you wanted to at least make an attempt to take care of them yourself."

The giant grimaced as he plucked a few metal shards from his face. "I appreciate the thought."

Sasha took aim at something in the corner of the room and fired. Sparks and smoke erupted and died after a brief but satisfying sizzle. "That was the last array." He turned to his companion. "I suppose she moved here to defend it. The hostile droids are still in action, but our teams must be close to shutting them down."

Wolfson shattered the sniper's rifle, removed her containers and pistol and destroyed them as well, then picked her up, placed her against the wall, and retrieved a net grenade. He held it against her and activated it to trap her there. "That means we only have a little more time to raise our tallies." He chuckled as the marksman joined him and they walked out of the warehouse. "What are you at?"

"Forty-two, with the sniper," Sasha replied and checked his rifle.

Wolfson laughed. "You need to catch up, Commander. I'm at fifty-six."

"Weren't you in a ship for a good chunk of the fight?"

He nodded and readied his shotgun as they drew closer to the central plaza. "Like I could keep count in that."

***

"He's here—heads down!" the infiltrator shouted. She, Magellan, and a few of the other hackers hunkered behind their chosen barrier as the back wall of the facility was hammered by cannon fire until it burst apart. Cyra and the bounty hunter looked around the machine that had sheltered them as a ship turned to present its side and a door opened. She helped the wounded man toward it. Julio reached the door and helped him into the vessel. "Thanks for coming."

"I'm glad to help." He scrutinized the patient. "Get your armor off. We'll patch you up and get you behind the lines."

"Just patch me up," Magellan stated. "We still need to get these droids offline."

Julio looked at Cyra in confusion. "I thought you did that already?"

She shook her head. "We shut their supply lines down, but—"

"Cyra?" Kit called over the comms. "I've found the main control for the droids."

She nodded to the other man, who dragged his passenger away as the door to the ship closed, and she walked back into the facility. "That's great news, Kit. I guess you need something on my end?"

"Some kind of command or password," she replied. "I assume it's a safety measure to make sure what we were planning wouldn't be so easy."

She found a console and began to search through different files. "It's a good thing we split up. How's the other plan coming along?"

"The droids and troops are making their way to the core. They were almost there when I last spoke to them," she stated. "Hopefully, we can finish this without blowing the place up, There's a lot of valuable tech in here."

"You'll get your chance," Chiyo stated and joined the comm. "And I've made my way to their storage center. I have direct access to almost all their files. Kaitō is currently sorting through them."

"That's equally great news!" Cyra cheered.

"Is Kaiden there with you?" Kit asked. "He raced off almost immediately after we set foot inside."

"He said he was going back to cover you."

Before the woman could reply that she hadn't seen him, a large explosion erupted in the hall leading to the core. Her map displayed Kaiden's dot in the hall with the other troops. "He works quickly."

A hacker flagged Cyra over and showed her a prompt. "Kit, I have it," she said and accepted a clearance command. "Can you shut them down now?"

The Azure Halo hacker chuckled. "Even better."

Wolfson backhanded an AO trooper who had moved a little too close and stamped on him as he blasted a second one in their chest. Vick and a few other Fire Riders pushed forward and dodged fire while they created a barrier, and more droids appeared from a few of the storage units. Sasha took aim from his perch but noticed some of the mechanicals had begun to stutter. Desmond, Janis, and Julio looked down from their ships and focused on the rapidly blinking lights amongst the robotic army.

The enemy droids powered down briefly and the AO troops seemed as confused as everyone else. The robots rebooted and as everyone readied to continue the fight, they turned to face any remaining Arbiter troops, their weapons at the ready.

The Riders, Kings, and everyone on the raiders side finally realized that the hackers had come through. Some asked for confirmation while others listened over the comms for details.

"This is Kit. We have command over the enemy droids," she announced channel-wide. As soon as reality settled amongst the fighters, there were cheers and hollers. The few remaining fighter ships rolled in celebration as they turned to find a landing area. Sasha lowered his rifle, took a deep breath, and jumped from his perch. He passed shouting and boisterous troops on his way to Wolfson, who held a couple of Arbiter soldiers at gunpoint.

"You should know it's over, right, boyos?" he asked, his head tilted and his expression smug. "We have questions for you, though, and we promise safety from our more... rowdy friends here if you promise to give us answers."

One of the soldiers kept his head down but the other looked up and his visor slid to the side. "That's not our choice to make," he said, his tone dull and without emotion. In the same moment, the two began to shake. Wolfson and Sasha readied their weapons as they took a step back.

"What the hell is going on?" the giant demanded.

"Look, Wolfson!" his friend exclaimed. All around the battlefield, the soldiers began to tremble and collapse and lights brightened along their armor.

"Everyone, back away!" the officer shouted, although most of the raiders had already begun to retreat. The soldiers' armor began to erupt and small explosions engulfed the field while the gang members took cover or sprinted to the gate. Even the already fallen soldiers weren't spared and their bodies joined the others as makeshift bombs.

It was over in minutes, but when the dust settled, even Sasha and Wolfson stood aghast and stared at the remains of the soldiers they had spoken to. "Suicide?" the officer finally asked, his voice gruff but shaken.

"It would seem to be," his friend muttered and holstered his rifle. "But by choice or design?"

Merrick finished his drink and shut down most of the monitors on which he'd watched the battle once the soldiers kill command was activated. He contacted the assassin. "There is no need to pursue, Dario. It's over for now. Return to base and we'll discuss our future actions. As for the Fenrir Base, I'll prepare it for disposal."

CHAPTER THIRTY-TWO

"Good God," Kaiden croaked as he crouched and raised his arms when the last of the droids guarding the core chamber was destroyed by AO soldiers suddenly exploding. He and the other troops stared at the fragmented robotic and body parts that slid noisily down the walls or rolled along the floor. Some looked at others, asking if they did it, but when they tried to defend themselves, he shook his head.

"It wasn't any of us," he announced. "It looked like some kind of failsafe or trigger maybe? I don't know what caused it."

"Maybe when the bots were compromised?" a King jockey suggested dubiously.

"It could have been." He glanced at a small camera in the corner next to the chamber door. "It could have been done remotely too."

"Hey," a Rider grunt muttered and waved a hand in front of his face. "Does it feel hotter to any of you?"

The ace straightened and he felt it as well—the same

kind of heat one would feel if they stood in front of a furnace or engine, and it felt as if was coming from the room beside them.

"Get the door open, Chief!" he ordered and bolted to the terminal.

"*Something is trying to push me out*," the EI stated. "*Wait, no...the paths are closing...the system is going offline.*"

The remaining lights in the hall went off to be replaced by emergency red glowstrips. "What's happening?"

"*I unlocked the door.*"

A few others joined him to grasp the edges of the large chamber doors and yank hard to slide them open. A blast of heat greeted them and cables uncoupled with loud hisses as the core grew brighter and the metal shell buckled. "Oh no," the ace whispered and slapped a hand to his helmet. "Chiyo, Cyra, Kit—"

"Kaiden, all the files are being deleted," Chiyo yelled. She and Kaitō tried hastily to download what they could as the petabytes of files and data began to vanish and the systems tried to cut her out.

"You have a worse problem than that," he responded urgently. "The core is overloading!"

"What?" Cyra shouted.

"I'm trying to stop it," Kit announced. "But nothing is accepted—dammit, my console crashed!"

"It's a purge," Chiyo deduced. "We need to evacuate."

"So much for our haul," the Halo hacker muttered and shouted to her men to grab what they could and retreat.

Kaiden also told the troops with him to get out. "Chiyo, we need to go."

"I can still get a little more," she protested.

"We have enough," he insisted. "Blueprints, pics—hell, we can take some of the robot scrap and show it around. We have to get out of the blast radius."

"We currently have almost a terabyte of information, madame," Kaitō confirmed. *"We can go over it in due course. I'm sure there is sufficient information that we can bring to light with this amount."*

She gritted her teeth and nodded as some of the servers behind her began to short out or spark. Reluctantly, she unhooked her gauntlet from the console and raced out of the room to catch up with Kit's team. "Cyra, where are you?"

"We jumped out of the hole Julio made," she explained, voice hitched and breathing heavy. "It was a rough landing, but we can get out through the back of the fort."

"We'll meet up later," Chiyo promised. "Kaiden, where are you?"

Her answer was a wall behind her imploding. Kaiden and a Rider heavy held their guns up and ushered the others through. "I didn't feel like making all those left turns," he explained. "Now, everyone, move your ass!"

Wolfson marched over with the enemy sniper hoisted over his shoulder while Zena watched the main building shake and rumble.

"What the hell is going on in there?" she demanded when small explosions erupted all over the building.

"They had a huge power spike," Fritz stated and glanced up from his holoscreen. "Kit, what the hell?"

"Someone activated the core remotely," she explained. "It's going to blow."

"What? Where are you?" Desmond demanded.

"Heading out of the building," Kaiden replied. "If we still have some dropships, we could use a lift."

"I'm on my way," Julio said and his ship took to the skies. Magellan frowned as he watched it bank toward the building.

"Same here. Meet you at the steps," Desmond stated as he pulled his ship around.

A number of larger explosions on the upper levels hurled rubble in all directions that troops retreating on the ground were forced to dodge or hurdle as they raced toward the gate.

"Well, those backfired," the bounty hunter muttered, believing his explosives were responsible.

Lycan drew in a deep breath and grimaced when a blare screeched and lights flashed red around him. It wasn't really a surprise to end up there. But, as his senses returned —without his muscle movement as yet—he realized that despite how loud and hot it was, he wasn't dead. He managed to roll onto his back and looked at the ceiling as the building shook and a series of blasts detonated some-where above him. He chuckled. No, he wasn't dead. Not yet, anyway.

Kaiden and the others reached the entrance and sprinted down the long hallway to the steps. Julio and Desmond's ships hovered in readiness. The doors opened and the thirty remaining troops and hackers scrambled in.

"Where's Cyra's team?" Julio asked as Chiyo and a hacker dragged Kaiden in.

"She escaped through the back," the infiltrator informed him as she pressed the switch to close the doors. He nodded, pulled the vessel up, and banked away from the building. Desmond followed.

All the troops and members of the assault had made it out of the fort, but that didn't stop their flight. The couple of hundred left either jumped inside any remaining shuttles or dropships or simply ran frantically across the mountainside as the stronghold began to collapse. Julio and Desmond flew up so no other ship was in their path and both boosted their vessels as the core finally reached its threshold and erupted. The force of the blast rattled their ships but they sustained no damage.

Dario sighed as the last of his visuals cut out. He shook his head and leaned back in his seat. Well, that seemed to be a waste. He looked at the remaining golem that still sat hunched over and paid close attention to the wall in front of it—a rather creepy hanger-on, he decided. His first inclination was to simply dissolve it, but Merrick might still have other uses for it and considering they had lost one of their bigger production facilities, perhaps it was best to hold on to the assets they had.

He received a notification on his tablet that the golem he had left in London had finally finished the download of its personality and orders. Morosely, he activated it and slid his tablet aside. He didn't get to finish his mission and the chance to face these raiders had slipped through his fingers. It was a bad day for him. He even saw Kaiden in the fray, along with other potential interests such as Baioh Wolfson and Sasha Chevalier, both decorated soldiers of the WC military. That could have been fun.

This would raise a few flags, of course. They might be able to stave off investigations and remain hidden for a while longer, but they couldn't rely on the relative safety of the shadows any longer. They would be forced to take more direct action now.

It really was a good thing Solos has his little toy. That would come in handy. For now, he would return to Italy and see how Merrick would deal with this new complication.

CHAPTER THIRTY-THREE

The raiders finally slowed as the last of the distant rumbles from the stronghold began to fade. Julio drifted into a slow descent. A few of the troops moved out of the way as the door to the dropship opened and Kaiden leapt out. He watched as jockeys helped each other out of their gear and soldiers checked on their teammates, either helping with wounds or congratulating one another. A group crowded around Zena and Fritz and he pushed his way through. "I'm glad to finally see you."

"You made one hell of an exit there." Fritz chuckled and offered his hand. "I haven't felt a rush like that since... Well, you were there."

He shook his hand and smiled, nodding to Zena. "You train your men well. It wouldn't have been nearly as smooth a fight without them."

"I would hardly have called all that smooth," she muttered before she gave a half-hearted shrug. "But we've trained hard since Ramses. I'm glad it's paid dividends."

"Any idea how many we lost? he asked.

"I haven't had the chance to do a headcount," Fritz admitted. "I know I saw a few go down and many more bots, but those are much easier to replace."

The ace nodded and stared at what remained of the base. "After a breather, we can go back and try to recover their bodies—or at least their tags if they had them." He glanced at the troops. "And, of course, you can take anything of interest."

"Assuming there's much left to take at this point," one of the Riders muttered.

"I'm...fairly sure that some of the warehouses and storage blocks should still be standing," he pointed. "Although I'll admit that the explosion probably spoiled most of the uh...spoils."

"You all should feel lucky to be able to grab whatever you can," Wolfson interjected sharply. The group turned as he and Sasha approached. The security officer had a person slung over his shoulder whom he promptly dropped once he reached them.

Kaiden removed his helmet and looked questioningly at the captured individual. "Who the hell is that?"

"A sniper Sasha and I had to deal with during the fight. She gave us a good run around and we went back for her after all the other soldiers spontaneously exploded."

"It was probably some kind of purge," Kit said as walked up behind the group with Chiyo, Desmond, and Magellan in tow. "A failsafe in case the facility was compromised."

"I guess we should consider ourselves fortunate that the droids didn't blow up as well," Zena muttered.

"Probably because Kit and Cyra already had control of

them," Fritz reminded her. "I'm certain that if the soldiers were wired to blow, you can bet the droids were."

The ace glanced quickly at Chiyo. "Cyra? That's right… Chiyo, did you hear from her? Did she make it out all right?"

She nodded but frowned slightly and held a tablet up. "She did. There was an open gate that allowed her and her team to get to a safe distance in the mountains, but she found something along the way." She handed the tablet to Sasha, although Kaiden, Wolfson, and the other leaders leaned in to see. It showed pictures of men and women in white coats and shirts sprawled over the forest floor, the back of their heads burst apart and bodies fallen in odd positions as if they had been shot in mid-sprint.

"Are these…the techs?" Kaiden asked.

The infiltrator nodded. "Techs, scientists, and other non-combat personnel. It would appear that even they weren't spared from the organization's failsafe."

"They've been able to remain hidden for so long because they are good at cleaning up after themselves—or at least making sure that any potential leaks were effectively plugged," Sasha stated and handed the tablet back. "They have been able to establish themselves by making everyone believe they are nothing more than fiction, but we have the means to force them out of hiding now." The commander turned to Chiyo. "Correct, Master Kana?"

She nodded and activated a holoscreen. "Kaitō is still sorting through everything we downloaded. Already, though, we have numerous documents detailing their technology developments, contracts, and conversations about business acquisitions, as well as many messages sent from the personnel to their benefactor."

"Singular?" Sasha asked.

Chiyo nodded. "There seem to be personal messages to other higher-ups and the like, but the senior officers and leaders of this facility all sent messages to one individual simply referred to as the leader. The correspondence is actually rather sparse when you narrow it down to only these particular messages. But there are dozens of references to the fact that they are doing everything for 'the mission' or the 'Arbiter project.'"

"There's still another possible source," Wolfson noted and looked at the prisoner. "We may be able to get more info from her but either way, the personal messages may be waved off by officials. The documents, contracts, and blueprints, however, will show that something was being planned—something that couldn't simply be accomplished by a couple of hundred idiots who acquired an old outpost."

The commander nodded. "We'll take this back to Nexus and have Laurie help you examine it. From there, we can take the case directly to the WC using my personal channels."

The trees around them stirred and a loud hum signaled the arrival of Janis' Zeppelin. Kit held a hand up and a holoscreen appeared. He smiled at the group. "I'm sorry for taking so long to contact all of you. I ended up drifting farther into the mountains than I realized after the drop."

"I'm glad to see you back safely, Janis," Kit responded.

"You missed most of the fun while you were loitering about." Fritz chuckled. "But I suppose I should be more impressed that you were able to keep that glorified floaty in the air so long."

"All of you should be impressed," Sasha stated and immediately drew the group's attention. "I'm not shrugging our losses off, but this could have gone much worse. Because everyone fought tooth and nail while accomplishing their objectives, we were spared that, even when certain developments arose out of our control."

"And now, it's our turn," Wolfson stated with a nod. "We'll make sure that this was only the beginning. This world may be full of a lot of idiots who need a good beating but now, we can at least make sure that the one who's been avoiding it so long finally gets theirs."

Zena straightened. "I assume the WC will take them on if all goes well, but then again, they are more reactive than proactive. They could drag their feet on this, even if you find something conclusive amongst it all." She tilted her head downward, her face solemn as if in thought. "I guess my offer still stands. They are a danger to us as much as anyone else. If you need anything, let me know. I can speak for me and my team, at least."

"Heh, are you trying to make me look bad?" Desmond snickered and thumped his chest. "The Kings and our ships are yours for the same reason, although we'll need time to get new ones and fix the ones we have."

"And the same for our droids. I believe all but a handful were left in the blast zone." Janis sighed. "Although they can be replaced. I recommend we head back and find some inspiration amongst the rubble."

Desmond smiled and returned to his ship. Zena shook

her head and left the group to order her team to head back to the fort to plunder what they could.

Kaiden watched them go for a moment. He turned to Wolfson and Sasha and nodded before he walked away. Chiyo followed him. "Are we heading back as well?"

"We have to pick Cyra up," he stated as he boarded Julio's ship.

"It would be a long walk back, wouldn't it?" She chuckled and sent a message to her friend that they were on their way.

"That, and she has the device we are supposed to get for Laurie," he reminded her with a smile. "We completed the mission and got what we came for, mostly. It would be a shame to fail the test after all that."

Merrick buried his face in his hands while his thoughts raced through his mind at a rapid pace. This rapid mental activity was normal for him in most circumstances, certainly, but there was an underlining uncertainty and confusion that was most uncommon.

They would have to speed their plans up, change the order, and tighten their focus. The battle made it very clear that they would no longer be afforded the time and ease they once had. Of course, the WC had been an unwitting ally of sorts and always brushed off anyone who brought up their existence or tried to look into the more under-hand dealings of the organization's various leaders as they laid the groundwork. Bribes and manufactured tragedies were equally important to their cause—and equally damning if their full extent were ever revealed.

It was possible that the raiders hadn't found enough evidence of their existence as a collective for the council to act in force. Perhaps they had only been able to ascertain that a number of companies had a stake in this outpost that dealt in unsanctioned development and research. Still, that would be enough for at least a few others to look deeper into it. That, in turn, would blossom into more investigations and potentially more attacks, and their advantage would only dwindle more rapidly. There were still pieces that needed to be put in place, but at this point, they might need to play the game with a handicap, at least until they could turn it to their favor.

Solos stated that he would begin his mission but that he had been unable to secure a foothold back in his company as yet. Apparently, the bounty hunter never came through. Although the count was clever—frighteningly so—the AO leader would have preferred he do this in a more traditional way. But he would have his end taken care of. Dario's little delivery would ensure it and that would buy them time to act and keep the WC at bay until they could take them on and win. To do that, however, they needed the right force.

He looked across his desk at a hologram of an island surrounded by a lake with numerous buildings and a vortex emblem mounted on the central monument. They would need troops and tech to make up for the amount they recently lost—and then to increase the numbers. They might have lost quantity but they could make up for it with quality. He stretched his hand and moved it through the hologram to break it apart.

They were an important piece and one he had relegated to later acquisition. But if certain members of Nexus were so eager to see the Arbiters come to light, they would oblige. He was sure they would fight, deny their mission, and try to push them back. But they would fail. Actually, no, they would succeed. While they might lose the victory they wanted, they would join them in their cause and achieve victory for the human race.

After all, that was their design.

Kaiden and friends are now available in audio at Amazon, Audible and iTunes. Check out book one, INITIATE, performed by Scott Aiello.

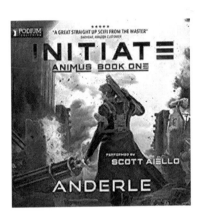

Check out book one at Amazon

(Book two is also available in audio, with more coming soon.)

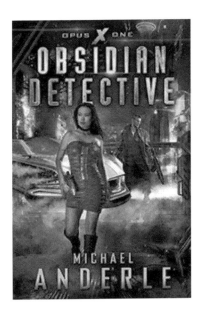

Pre-order now to have the book arrive on your Kindle November 1st.

Two Rebels whose Worlds Collide on a Planetary Level.
On the fringes of human space, a murder will light a fuse and send two different people colliding together.

She lives on Earth, where peace among the population is a given. He is on the fringe of society where authority is how much firepower you wield.

She is from the powerful, the elite. He is with the military.

Both want the truth – but is revealing the truth good for society?

Two years ago, a small moon in a far off system was set to be the location of the first intergalactic war between humans and an alien race.

It never happened. However, something was found many are willing to kill to keep a secret.

Now, they have killed the wrong people.

How many will need to die to keep the truth hidden?

As many as is needed.

He will have vengeance no matter the cost. *She will dig for the truth. No matter how risky the truth is to reveal.*

Coming November 1st from Amazon and other Digital Book Stores

AUTHOR NOTES - MICHAEL

SEPTEMBER 10, 2019

"The Author would say thank you for reading this book… If the Author was around." John turned around. He was standing on the sidewalk, the trees shading the street down both sides as he tried to find the voice amongst the shrubs in old Ms. Benjamin's yard.

"Come again?" He spoke aloud.

"I said," the voice replied. John looked down. At his feet, about as high as his Converse high tops, was a small …

Fairy? *A lawn fairy?* He got closer then kneeled. He then noticed the razor-sharp teeth. The fairie continued speaking. "That the author would have said *thank you* for reading the book."

"What book?"

"Unbelievable Mr. Brownstone."

John thought about it. "I haven't read a Brownstone since … Uh… He got married to Shae. Last I read was the latest Animus." John didn't like the look on the little guy's face. "Did I miss one?"

"You missed *two*, actually." He put his hands on his hips, looking up. "You call yourself a reader?"

"I've been busy. You know," John jerked a thumb to his blue Nike backpack, "College."

"Not an acceptable excuse," the small fairy answered. "In fact, there is no excuse. It's what we told the Author before we had our final negotiation. He promises he won't be tardy again."

"Whatevs," John stood up. "I've got to go, I'll get to it when I get to...OUCH!" John's hand swept down, meeting his foot he was lifting as he slapped the little guy off of his ankle, rocketing him into the grass.

There was blood running down, soaking his sock. "Dude, why the hell did you bite me?" he asked as John noticed the little guy, a maniacal grin on the tiny face wiping a bit of skin and meat out of his mouth climbing out of the grass to get on the sidewalk.

"How the hell did you get such a big chunk out of my foot, ya ass?" John kneeled, moving his sock to catch more of the blood.

"Dinner shouldn't call me names..." the little fairy hissed, his voice going up an octave.

"Dinner?" John looked over to him, "I'm not your dinner you little masochistic mosquito. I'm a hundred times your size and..." John noticed the tall grass starting to move around in Ms. Benjamin's lawn. Like something – or several somethings - was coming through it. "I'm uh..."

"You...are...*dinner*." The fairy smiled once more, showing the red coloring of his teeth. John's blood. "At least the Author was smart enough to negotiate. You just called me names..."

John jumped up, turned, and sprinted away.

Forty-five minutes later, a dog was sniffing a blue back-pack just five houses down, laying on the sidewalk…

John was nowhere to be seen.

WE HAVE TWO MORE ANIMUS BOOKS COMING…
Don't let the Lawn Fairies catch you missing one.
Once they finish with John, you might be next…

If you haven't read
The Unbelievable Mr. Brownstone,
we suggest you try it.

If you have read all of
The Unbelievable Mr. Brownstone,
and all of Animus…
You are safe.

For now.

CONNECT WITH THE AUTHORS

Michael Anderle Social
   Website:
   http://lmbpn.com

Email List:
   http://lmbpn.com/email/

Facebook Here:
   https://www.facebook.com/OriceranUniverse/
   https://www.
facebook.com/TheKurtherianGambitBooks/
   https://www.facebook.com/groups/
320172985053521/ (Protected by the Damned Facebook
Group)

48165519R00164

Printed in Poland
by Amazon Fulfillment
Poland Sp. z o.o., Wrocław